T0294313

NEW HOPE

by R.J. Bonett

ISBN: 978-1-09830-165-1

eBook ISBN: 978-1-09830-166-8

Disclaimer: This is a work of fiction. All the characters and events are purely fictional. Businesses, locations and organizations while real- are used in a way that is purely fictional.

Cover Design: Ronald J. Bonett

Grateful appreciation to: Marie Bonett, & Bonnie Hilfiger, for content approval.

Editor: Rachel Heitzenrater

Introduction

Allen Simpson, a playwright with a few successful local productions wants to make a change from writing plays to acting. His thoughts being, "If I can write a script, why not attempt playing one of the characters?" Trying to fulfill that commitment, in the fall of 1975 he sought a part in a play. He'd been trying for several years without success, and being almost 40, was wondering whether it's still worth the effort, but decides to give it one last try.

He's drawn to New Hope, a small town 30 miles north of Philadelphia along the bank of the Delaware River. The town claims its reputation through artists, folk singers and the very popular New Hope Theatre.

To ensure its location the night before his audition, he entered the parking lot that rainy November evening. A flash of lightening illuminated the sign on the wall of the converted grist mill that read *New Hope Theatre-The Players*. The way it was worded sent mixed signals to his brain. Was it because of the success of people advancing to the New York stage and beyond, or just a farewell to those like himself who tried?

Looking for a place to stay, he happened on a bed and breakfast where several aspiring actors were lodging, trying out for the same play.

With his final attempt at acting, the title of the play was *Murder at the Logan Mansion*. Little did he realize he would be involved in a real-life drama, which included anger, jealousy, love and *MURDER!*

Chapter 1

The rain-slick parking lot was as empty as my success trying to find a job after the expense of dramatics school. The Granite Stone Grist Mill that stood before me was several hundred years old and had been converted into a theatre. With the occasional flash of lightning, the sign on the side of the building boldly read *New Hope Theatre- The Players*. The way it was worded sent mixed signals to my brain. Was it because of the success of people advancing to the New York stage and beyond, or just a farewell to those like myself who tried? I wasn't sure, but I've never been a quitter. However, the lack of success the last two years trying to land a position as an actor was beginning to challenge that boast. After writing several short scripts for plays, I decided to give acting a try.

The theatre is part of the re-birth of New Hope, a small town on the bank of the Delaware River 30 miles above Philadelphia. It came into existence as a stopover on the Erie Canal in the early 1800, part of it still existing today. It's become a popular attraction, riding in a barge drawn along the canal by mule.

The town has one major thoroughfare lined with shops of all kinds, from art to handmade jewelry. In fact, it's become an art lover's mecca for at least 30 years.

These are the people who actually began its rebirth. Upscale restaurants soon followed taking advantage of the opportunity, bringing in more and more people with diverse economic backgrounds. The weekends brought crowds making it hard pressed to find a parking space, and you could see every different kind of vehicle from motor cycles to Mercedes.

If I was successful landing this job, it would be my home as long as the theatre troop felt my acting skills were worthy.

At almost 40 years of age, I often wondered why I hadn't started on my quest 15 years sooner.

Now that I knew the location of the theatre, I had to seek a place to spend the night. It was only 8:30. Being November, it was already past the tourist season and I knew it wouldn't be difficult to find one. Off the main thoroughfare were numerous signs of vacancies on various houses advertising bed and breakfast establishments. Pulling up in front of a late 19th century Victorian, I decided to give it a try. After knocking, the porch light went on, and I could see a shadow opening the inner vestibule door. Stepping back, a woman who looked to be in her early 70s opened the front door. Short, with white hair tied in a bun on the back of her head, she wore a dark blue house dress with small white flowers. The white hand-knitted shawl she had over her shoulders complimented her appearance of what anyone would describe as a grandmother.

"Can I help you, young man?"

"Yes, I'd like to rent a room for at least two nights."

"I don't recall seeing your face. Have you stayed here before?"

"No Ma'am. I'm new in town. I'm supposed to have an audition at the New Hope Theatre tomorrow afternoon."

After looking me up and down, judging my sincerity, she said, "Well, step inside. These November rains are cold and damp."

"Yes, I know," I shook off the excess rain from my jacket before stepping in.

"How much are your rooms?"

"Since it's off-season and you're alone, it will be $30 per day. That includes breakfast. Lunch is on your own. If you want dinner, it can be arranged with a morning notice in advance. That will be an extra $5 dollars."

"That's fine. I just might as well tell you now. I'm in for dinner both nights."

"Good. I'll show you to your room. What's your name?"

"Allen. Allen Simpson. And yours?"

"Ethel Devlin." Thinking to myself, "Even the name fits with her appearance."

"Mrs. Devlin, could you wait one moment while I run to the car and get my overnight bag?" Opening the door, I made a mad dash to the car retrieving it then returned.

Climbing the stairs to the second floor, I could hear voices from inside several rooms. The number on each door indicated there were five rental rooms on that floor. We continued down the hall.

"Your room is up here, young man."

She led me to another set of stairs that went to the third floor. I suspected it would be an attic with old items carefully preserved for any latecomer, but upon opening the door, I was surprised. The room was beautifully furnished with an all Victorian motif. I knew I could be comfortable here. Thinking to myself, "If they give me a script, I'll be able to do it without disrupting any other guests." I was looking forward to the room for the next two days. Settling in for the night, I felt comfortable with my surroundings, and quickly fell asleep.

***

I awoke early to movement and conversations in the hall on the second floor. Opening my door, I could smell the aroma of freshly brewing coffee coming from the kitchen. Fortunately for me, there was a bathroom on my floor that no one else seemed to be aware of, and I was able to get showered and dressed for breakfast without interruption. Getting to the dining room, Mrs. Devlin was busy arranging plates and silverware for breakfast.

"Good morning, Mrs. Devlin. I'll trade favors with you."

She looked at me inquisitively.

"I'll finish setting the table for a cup of that coffee," I said.

She smiled. "Young man, that's a deal. Where would you like to sit at the table?"

I placed the silverware where I was standing. "Right here will be fine."

Retreating to the kitchen, she returned with a carafe of coffee. Smiling, she conveniently placed it in front of where I chose to sit. With a wink and a nod, I graciously thanked her. Within a half hour, the other guests began filing into the room. Taking seats, they noticed I was a new face amongst them.

"Good morning!" I said, "My name is Allen Simpson. I arrived late last evening."

A middle-aged man taking seats with his wife replied, "I'm Joe Cartwright, and this is my wife Sarah. We're just passing through on our way to Boston."

Another man in a business suit announced bluntly, "I'm John. I'm here on business."

Another middle-aged couple came to the table and identified themselves as Mr. and Mrs. Green. The last two seats were taken by a man in his mid-20s and a woman who appeared to be in her early 30s.

The man was 5'10", thin build, with long, blond hair tied in a pony tail, with an earring on his right ear. With very handsome features, he was dressed in casual clothes and announced without elaborating, "I'm Peter Austin."

The woman was extremely attractive, about 5'4", shapely, with long, auburn hair tied back with a light brown ribbon. "I'm Roselyn Carter," she extended her hand across the table. "I have no secrets. I'm trying to get a position at the New Hope Theatre."

Taken by her bluntness, I said, "That's coincidental, Miss Carter. I'm here for the same purpose. Here, let me pour you some coffee."

"Thank you." Appearing to have the same mutual interest, she asked, "What time is your audition?"

"I was told to be there at ten this morning. What time is yours?"

"I was told to be there at 1 p.m."

"I wonder why the time difference? I hope there isn't that many people trying out. Have you had any previous experience Miss Carter?"

"I had a small part in a play at an L.A. dinner theatre, but I hardly think that's enough to be a shoe-in for a part."

"You're from California then?"

"No, I'm actually from Iowa a small town no one knows exists." Pointing to her right, she said, "Peter and I were enrolled in dramatics class at Berkley."

"Are you both trying out for a part?"

"Yes."

I continued, "I was hoping they'd give me a manuscript I could study before the tryout."

Peter remarked sarcastically, "From what I read about the review, you look to be too old for any of the parts."

Breaking the potential confrontation, Mrs. Devlin brought the food to the table. "Enjoy. How many can I expect back for dinner tonight?"

"I'll be here," I quickly replied.

"I know. You told me last night. Who else?"

Mr. and Mrs. Green said yes and Roselyn also replied to the affirmative.

"Will you be here, Peter?"

"I don't know yet, Mrs. Devlin. I can't say for sure."

"Well, make up your mind before you leave this morning."

Roselyn asked, "Allen, have you ever had any experience other than dramatics school?"

"On stage no, but I've written a few short scripts that were somewhat successful locally. Not to boast, but I thought if I can write a script, maybe it wouldn't be very hard to portray one of the characters."

Peter again sarcastically replied, "Well, first you should study the characters of the play before deciding to try out for a part."

Roselyn replied, "Well Peter, don't judge all failures by our attempts. I say, Allen, go for it."

You could see in Peter's face he was taken aback by Roselyn's remark, as if he was a scolded child.

Mrs. Green entered the conversation. "You young people are interesting."

"Why's that Mrs. Green?" Roselyn asked.

"Well, when we were young, we thought the place where we lived was everything. Today, people just travel around like vagabonds and seem to enjoy being unsettled."

John the businessman looked at her remarking, "That's what they have to do to get recognized. I'd love to join your conversation, but unfortunately, I don't have time." Looking at his watch he hurriedly rose from his chair, "Thank you Mrs. Devlin, for a great stay. If I'm ever back this way, I'll be sure to stop."

"Thank you, Mr. Thomas. You travel safely."

"Thank you. I will."

Upon his departure, Roselyn resumed the conversation. "Mrs. Green, the reason I came all the way to the East Coast is the lack of competition here.

Everyone aspiring to be an actress or an actor like Peter and I are a dime a dozen in L.A. We came here with the hopes we could get recognized by someone close to the New York City Theatre Guild. I heard someone say they visit this area frequently."

"Well, dear, for your sake, I hope this is your lucky day."

"Thank you, Mrs. Green. Now if everyone will excuse me, I'd like to return to my room."

Shortly after Roselyn left, Peter followed. In 10 minutes, I excused myself, and as I was passing Roselyn's door, I could hear Peter in her room. It sounded like a discussion about his attitude at the table. Continuing down the hall, I returned to my own room to get a light jacket before leaving.

Looking out the window, the leaves on the maple trees were a brilliant yellow. Being wet from the night before enhanced their color, and the wet bark appeared black. The contrast was magnificent.

Going down the stairs, I caught part of the continuing conversation between Roselyn and Peter. As she was leaving the room, she bluntly remarked over her shoulder at his continued conversation, "I'll see you tonight."

Seeing me in the hall, she asked, "Are you leaving for your appointment?"

"Yes, I thought I'd walk to the theatre. I'm early, but it seems like a beautiful day."

"Do you mind if I walk with you?"

"No, I enjoyed your company at breakfast, but aren't you going to be a little early for your audition?"

"Yes, I just wanted to get away from Peter for awhile. He carries that air of stuffy sophistication so many Californians suffer from. It gets the best of him sometimes. Other than that, he's a pretty good egg."

"Then if I'm not being too forward, are you two an item?"

Looking inquisitive at my question, she asked with raised eyebrows, "Do you mean are we engaged or married or living together or something? No. In fact, he has an interest in me I don't want any part of. Not that Mrs. Devlin would let us share the same room being unmarried, but I won't let him share my room."

"What do you mean by that?"

She tried to turn my attention away from the conversation and remarked, "I love this part of the country. The fall colors when the leaves turn, the beauty of it all."

I decided to drop the conversation in favor of talking about our aspirations.

"I'm about 20 minutes early for the audition," I said, "That looks like a quaint little coffee shop. Care to join me?"

"I'd like to. I thought this light sweater would be warm enough, but the breeze off the river is a little cooler than I expected."

After getting the coffee, we sat at stools along the front window. It was a typical coffee shop, straight from the era of Greenwich Village, with folk art and the like adorning the walls. Looking out the window, I could see Peter looking up and down the street, as if he was searching for Roselyn.

"He must be looking for you. I'll get him." As I stood up, she tugged at my jacket sleeve.

"Don't bother."

I began to wonder if that was why she cut my questions short. Was there something more to this on his part than just trying to be aspiring actors?"

We watched through the window as he gave up his search, heading in the direction of the theatre. Waiting about ten minutes, I finally looked at my watch.

"Roselyn, I have to go. I don't want to be late."

"Good luck. I'll see you later today."

"Aren't you coming?"

"No, I think I'll just take in some of these shops and see what they have to offer."

Chapter 2

Arriving at the theatre, I opened the door to a few people seated several rows back from the stage. They seemed to be the people giving auditions. I approached them asking, "I was supposed to speak to someone about a part in the play. Can you tell me who's in charge?"

Just then, the person on stage began reciting lines from a manuscript. Not wanting to interrupt, I took a seat behind them. Within several minutes, a woman who was part of a four-person reviewing panel stood and remarked to the young girl on stage, "Sharon, that part has to be recited with more drama. Someone has just told you your mother died. Maybe you need more time to rehearse that part."

"Excuse me for interrupting. My name is Allen Simpson. I'm here for an audition for the play."

The panel consisting of three women and one man quickly turned around. The woman I was addressing was in her early 40s, brown hair and attractive by any standards of a woman that age.

"I'm Florence Stark. I'm the playwright and director. I've read one of your pieces several years ago. I was impressed. If you're a playwright, why are you here for an audition?"

"I thought I would try being involved in the theatre from another point of view."

She nodded as if she were saying good luck, not completely reassuring that I would be successful.

Maybe it was my skepticism failing so many times, but I couldn't let that get in the way. Turning to look at me, she introduced the other three people she was seated with.

"This is Charles Cohen. He's a critic and financier of the play."

New Hope

Charles was in his early 50's, thin, about 5'7", with a receding gray hairline. "This is Jan Doherty. She's in charge of costumes and stage positioning."

Jan was a truly beautiful woman in her mid 20s. Her long, auburn hair was tied up in a bun on top of her head, with a pencil protruding from it. Even under a loose-fitting heavy knit sweater, I could see she was well-built. Taking the pencil and flipping it back and forth between her fingers, she seemed to be eyeing me for clothing, as if I was already successful with the audition. That seemed encouraging.

I extended my hand and said, "I'm pleased to meet you."

Florence continued. "This is Cheryl Freeman. She's an actress who will be in the play. Cheryl is like a permanent fixture here at the theatre. She's been in several productions."

She too was a pretty woman in her late 20s, with long black hair.

She replied, looking at Florence saying, "Don't let her fool you. I just come cheaper in cost than anyone else. That's why I've been in a few productions. If you work as cheaply as I do, you'll be a shoe-in."

Extending her hand to shake mine, Florence remarked, "If you succeed with the audition, she'll be more than happy to help you develop your part."

"That's true, as long as you don't try to outperform me."

A light laughter came from the group.

"Well, now that I've met my panel, where do I go from here?" I asked.

Florence thumbed through a few folders finding the part I was obviously supposed to audition for handing it to me. After opening it, I asked, "Am I supposed to recite something now, or may I take this with me to rehearse?"

Florence abruptly replied, seemingly still focused on the person auditioning on stage, "We'll see you at 1:30."

Feeling relieved I had time to rehearse. I was making my exit when I heard Florence say. "Ok. Bring in the next person auditioning for the part of the maid."

Looking over my shoulder, I could see Cheryl still looking at me as I was ready to push open the door. With the bright sun shining in, it illuminated a dark part of the seating area, and something caught my eye in the last few rows. I could see a person slunk down in one of the seats. It looked like Peter. He must have been watching and listening to my conversation with

Florence and the group.

Pretending not to notice him, I made my exit. Getting outside, I looked at my watch. Realizing I had several hours before returning, I hurried back to my room to rehearse.

Going inside, I met Mrs. Devlin at the bottom of the stairs.

"Excuse me, Mrs. Devlin. They gave me part of the manuscript in the role I'm trying out for. If I wouldn't be any bother to you, could I practice the lines in my room?"

"Allen, there's no one else here to disturb at present. Practice to your heart's content."

Realizing she may have given me more liberties than she should have, she continued, "That is, if it doesn't have a part with shouting in it."

As I passed Roselyn's room, she surprised me when she opened the door.

"Allen. So they threw you a life preserver, letting you practice your part before this afternoon."

"That's a good way to put it. Mrs. Devlin said no one else was here."

"I guess she was busy in the kitchen when I came in. Is the part you have a much younger person as Peter suggested?"

"I only briefly looked at it, but I don't think so. I better get cracking memorizing these lines."

"Good luck!" She closed the door to her room once again.

Opening the manuscript, I began to read. The play was titled, *"Murder at the Logan Mansion."*

The second page revealed the names of the characters, and their relevance to the production. Quickly scanning the page, there was a character that suited my age to a T. Closing the manuscript briefly, I thought about Peter saying there wasn't a character my age in the play. Was he jealous that I might somehow get the part over him? I couldn't worry about that now. I had better things to do with my time.

Looking over the story, it was about a murder that takes place at an estate.

The part I was trying out for was the owner, Larry Cranston, a married man with an infatuation for a dance instructor working there. My wife's part, Sylvia Cranston, was surprisingly enough penciled in- Cheryl Freeman.

There were two other characters with major roles, and that was my wife's alcoholic brother Tony, and another that I assumed was the role of the dancing instructor, but there was no name penciled in after them. I immediately assumed that part was being pursued by Roselyn.

There were several other main characters: a police detective, the butler and chauffer which hadn't been selected yet.

A gardener had a small part. His name was Wally Williams, played by Edward Heart, and the maid being auditioned as I entered the theatre was Sharon Fox, being played by Jennifer Grimes. Their names were penciled in already alongside their characters.

Looking at the characters, I tried to imagine Peter only being able to fill in for my wife's alcoholic brother Tony. He couldn't possibly fit the mold of the police detective and wouldn't look right playing the role of a butler, chauffer possibly. But would he accept a lesser role?

Giving it enough thought, I put it aside to memorize my script and began to read some of the lines aloud. Just then I heard a light knock on the door. Opening it, Roselyn was standing there.

"I heard you reciting your lines. Is there anything I can do to help?"

"I didn't think I was loud enough to disturb anyone."

Looking around the room, she repeated, "You're not. Is there anything I can do to help?"

Opening the door wider, uninvited, she stepped in.

"If you care to listen, you're more than welcome."

Beginning again, she sat in a chair listening intently, studying my gestures while I recited several lines.

"Allen, not to give you a big head, but I see nothing wrong with the way you delivered those lines. Whether it's good or bad to someone who's selecting the players is something I can't tell, but you acted exactly the way they teach dramatics at Berkley."

"That's encouraging." I was about to continue, when there was a second knock at the door. Thinking I was reciting too loudly, I opened it expecting to see Mrs. Devlin, but instead, Peter was standing there.

"Is Roselyn here?"

I didn't have to answer his question. He could see her sitting in a chair.

"Roselyn, I thought you would help me with my lines."

"I was just helping Allen with his. Where have you been all morning? I could have been helping you."

"I went for a walk."

"Did you go to the theatre?"

Not realizing I saw him there, he replied, "No."

"So you two have manuscripts already?" I asked.

"Yes, we picked them up yesterday. I'm trying out for the role of the dance instructor, Carol Wilson, and Peter's seeking the role of Tony Cappolla, Sylvia Cranston's alcoholic brother."

I avoided any conversation about either of their roles and didn't want to start an incident about not being able to fit into one, as Peter suggested earlier.

"Well, I won't hold you two back. Thanks for the input, Roselyn," I said.

After they left, I resumed practicing my lines. The thought of Peter lying about not going to the theatre kept coming to the forefront. Why did he feel he had to lie about it?

Before I realized, it was already 1 p.m. Hurrying down the stairs I met Roselyn and Peter in the hallway. I said, "I guess we'll all be given a chance to show our skills this afternoon?"

Peter sarcastically remarked, "I hope the role is not too difficult for you."

Roselyn replied, "Well Peter, we haven't been the success we thought we'd be either. Let's not get too confident."

***

Arriving at the theatre, we checked in with Miss Stark, the director. The same panel was there as this morning, minus Jan, the costumes and stage positioning director.

Florence asked, "Which one of you would like to go first?"

Looking at each other for a few moments, wondering who was going to take the plunge, Sharon, who I met this morning as a fixture in the theatre replied,

"If someone doesn't make the move, the play will have already run. Who'll go first?"

Roselyn volunteered and as she climbed the stairs to the stage, everyone took seats to observe.

New Hope

Miss Stark called out, "Ok Roselyn, let me hear the part where you tell Mr. Cranston you think you shouldn't continue being his dance instructor."

With all the professional ability she could muster, she began her lines, physically acting the gestures as she was saying them. "Larry, I don't know whether I should continue being your instructor. I feel this relationship is getting too close. Maybe you should hire someone else."

"That's good, Roselyn. That's exactly the way I want you to play the part. I know without all the stage settings it's more difficult to act out the scene, but you did very well."

Seeing her opening a copy of the play, I assumed she penciled Roselyn's name beside the character.

"Ok, Peter, your next."

"Let's take it from when you put your foot in the doorway. Remember, you're intoxicated, wanting to have sex with Sharon the maid."

Acting out, staggering to his room, then re-emerging, he acted the part of knocking at Sharon's door.

"Sharon, why don't you come to my room for a nightcap?"

Florence called out, "OK, she turns you down. Then what?"

"I put my foot in the doorway and force my way in."

"Well, don't tell me. Act out the part."

After acting it, Miss Stark said, "Ok, you're in. Now what?"

"In a drunken stupor, I try making advances to her. She resists my advances, and I push her down on the bed. I hold a pillow over her face to stifle her loud voice, and she stops moving."

"OK, act out the part where you realize she's not moving and was dead."

Watching intently, he acted out the part to perfection. I thought, "If I could do as well, that would be great."

"Ok Peter, you did well." She took her pencil, and I assumed she jotted his name next to the part. At that moment, Jan, the person in charge of position and costumes entered the theatre.

Getting to where we were seated; she asked, "Peter: would you mind cutting your hair and dying it for the production?"

"Well, if it's absolutely necessary, no."

"We have two more people auditioning for that part this afternoon, think about it."

Realizing they weren't fixed on him playing the role, Florence said, "Ok Allen, you're next. After I took the stage, she said,

"I know you just got the script several hours ago, so give it your best shot. You're in your rec room being taught how to dance, when you let Carol the dance instructor, know you care for her."

Just then, Mr. Cohen, the play's financier entered the theatre. Hearing what was asked of me he loudly remarked, "Just act natural, and tell her the next dance instruction should be in your bedroom."

A light chuckle came from the group.

"OK, Allen, you can continue."

With all the effort I could muster I began to recite my lines. Pretending to look down on the face of the imaginary dance partner while whirling with the motion of pretend music, I recited the few lines I memorized. Pausing after I was finished, I added a little humor, by bowing to the imaginary dance instructor and said, "Thank you for the dance, you're so light on your feet."

It brought a laugh from my critics, as they put their heads together evaluating my performance. I held my breath, waiting for a negative response like the ones I received several times in the past. Suddenly, I saw some nodding of heads, which was encouraging.

Florence humorously remarked, "OK Allen, you and your partner can get the full manuscript."

It brought a much-needed relief to my wait and a few laughs from the critics. Happily taking the manuscript, Cheryl, the actress that would play the part of my wife, congratulated me.

"I'll look forward to working with you. If there's any question about our scenes, we can practice them in the theatre for the next several days before going into production."

"I'd like that. I'm staying at a bed and breakfast on Canal Street. The address is 212. Mrs. Ethel Devlin's the proprietor. Not to be too demanding, when can we start?"

"Tomorrow if you like, I think the auditions will be completed today. Shall we meet here?" she asked.

"There's a coffee shop on Main Street we could meet there, are you familiar with it?""

"She replied, "I've been there a hundred times. I'll see you then, between 9:00 and 10:00.

"Ok?"

Returning to the house, Mrs. Devlin met me in the hall. "Well how did your audition go?"

"I got the part. I was going to ask about extending my residency for awhile."

"If you want to continue, I'll make the stay $150 a week, including dinner. How's that sound?"

"Not knowing how long the show will run, that sounds fine. Has Roselyn returned?"

"Yes, I heard her speaking to Mrs. Green about getting her part. How about Peter?"

"They didn't tell him he was successful when I was there. They still had several more people to audition."

As I was passing Roselyn's room, her door opened. "Congratulations, Allen, I knew you would get the part."

"Yes, I was a little worried when they seemed to go into conference, but when Florence nodded her head and Mr. Cohen seemed to agree, I felt relieved. Now all I have to do is study the script."

"I don't think you'll have a problem with that."

"I hope not. Cheryl offered to practice with me at the theatre tomorrow. I'm meeting her in the morning at the coffee shop where we were this morning."

"What time is that?"

"I told her I'd meet her between 9 and 10."

"Do you think she would mind me coming along? I really need a different place to rehearse."

"I shouldn't think that will be a problem- I'll see you at dinner. I want to spend as much time studying as possible."

Climbing the stairs to the third floor, I heard Peter's voice in the hall below and stopped to listen.

"Roselyn: congratulations on getting your part. I still don't know whether I got mine yet. If I don't, what do you intend to do?"

"What's that supposed to mean?"

"Well, I assumed we would move on and try somewhere else."

"Peter, we're not attached by an umbilical cord. I've been traveling with you for several months trying to land a job. This is my chance."

"Are you sure it's just the job your concerned with?"

She replied, "What is it with you and this fixation with some sort of relationship between us? I thought I made myself clear when we started out this quest for fame. There's nothing to it and will never be. I appreciate you helping me finance the adventure, but if you think it lays claim on my affections, you're wrong. If you'll excuse me, I have to rehearse my lines."

"Can I come in and help you?"

"No, I think I'd rather do it alone."

It was the end of their conversation, and I could hear Roselyn's door close. I realized why they were traveling together, and it dispelled my opinion of a relationship with one another.

After several hours of going over the script, I returned to the dining room for dinner. We began to get into light conversation about the events of the day, when Peter came into the room.

Mrs. Devlin asked, "Peter, you didn't tell me you would be here for dinner. If your name wasn't in the pot for it this morning, I can't accommodate you."

"That's Ok Mrs. Devlin. I'm going out to dinner with someone."

"Well, enjoy your evening."

After he left, the conversation picked up where it left off. Mrs. Green seemed fascinated with our attempt to get noticed for the roles we were assigned and began asking a lot of questions. At one point Mr. Green had to remind her, her dinner was getting cold.

Over coffee, our interest in the play became a two-way conversation between Roselyn and me.

After dinner, we retired to our different rooms to continue practicing our parts.

Around 10, I heard Peter once again in the hall below. I opened my door and listened to a conversation between him and Roselyn.

I heard her say, "What are you doing, practicing the part of the drunken brother of Sylvia? If you are, you'll be a shoe-in for the part. Practicing it outside my door instead of the stage just might get you evicted by Mrs. Devlin. Lower your voice."

"I know I'm a little drunk, but who wouldn't be after getting the rejections I got today, first from the theatre, then from you."

"You mean you haven't secured a part?"

"I don't know yet. Why, are you concerned?"

"I just thought I'd ask. I think you better call it a night and get to bed."

Hearing the door close, it seemed to be the end of the conversation.

***

Peter was absent from breakfast in the morning, and was no wonder from his condition last night.

Mrs. Devlin commented, "Roselyn, I heard you and Peter in the hall last night. I can't have the other guests being disturbed," she began to continue when Roselyn interrupted.

"Mrs. Devlin, I'm truly sorry. I'll make sure it doesn't happen again."

She mumbled as she returned to the kitchen, and the only distinguishable words you could hear were, "It better not!"

"Roselyn, I was coming from my bathroom when I heard Peter knock at your door. If Mrs. Devlin has any question that you didn't start it, tell her to ask me."

I looked at my watch. "Roselyn, it's 9 o'clock. If we're going to meet Cheryl, we should get going."

Taking her last sip of coffee replied, "I'll get my manuscript and meet you at the front door."

Chapter 3

Arriving at the coffee shop, we met Cheryl. Her facial expression told me she seemed surprised that Roselyn was with me, but didn't comment.

She said, "Are we ready?"

"Yes, I think we're ready to be taught by a pro."

Promptly replying with a grin, "I wouldn't say that, but this play does seem like it will be fun. There are humorous parts and serious parts. It's more like a spoof rather than a serious murder story."

Roselyn replied, "Well, I guess the paying audience will determine the length of time it will run. Cheryl, have they chosen anyone to play your alcoholic brother? If not, I have a good candidate. He came in that way last night."

"Yes, I know." Catching herself in the middle of her statement, she quickly changed the subject.

Roselyn and I looked at each other. Her statement inadvertently told us who Peter dined with last evening. It was her.

We walked to the theatre and when we got there, the door was unlocked. Florence was already there with Jan discussing the costumes and prop positioning on the stage.

Cheryl remarked, "Good morning, I assumed we would be alone today?"

Florence replied, "We're only going to be about an hour. Then it's all yours."

The three of us sought out a quiet corner, and discussed different techniques of delivering our lines. Within the hour, Florence left, and Jan stayed behind.

"You don't mind if I watch you rehearsing for awhile, do you?" she asked.

I replied, "No, that is, I don't. I can't answer for these two."

Looking at Roselyn with approval, Cheryl answered, "It's fine with us."

Taking positions on the stage, we began with the scene where Cheryl, playing the role of my disgruntled wife Sylvia, accuses me of an infatuation with the dance instructor she hired, Carol Wilson, played by Roselyn.

Cheryl began her lines. "I know you're infatuated with Carol. I should have known better than to hire someone so young and attractive."

"Well, dear, you're the one that insisted I learn how to do it. Why didn't you hire someone old and decrepit? Or better yet, buy one of those patterns for the floor with the printed foot-prints I could follow- you know, from Arthur Murray or Fred Astaire. In fact, why bother at all this late in our marriage?"

Cheryl remarked, "Allen, be more nonchalant with your remarks, not so serious. This is supposed to be one of the less serious parts."

"Ok, let me try again. "Well dear, you're the one who insisted I learn how to do it!"

I walked across the imaginary room and turned. "Why didn't you hire someone old and decrepit?" I shrugged my shoulders. "Or buy one of those patterns for the floor. You, know, the ones with printed foot-prints I could follow from Arthur Murray or Fred Astaire. In fact, why bother at all at this late stage in our marriage."

"Allen, that's good! The way you casually walked across the room, the slowly turning saying your lines. It was especially effective when you gave your shoulders a shrug when you said, 'Why bother at this late stage in our marriage.' Anyone can recite lines. It's acting out the parts that are the keys to success."

"Actually I got it from you when you said your lines. Your movements help me create the scene."

"That's exactly right. That's why it's important to interact with the people you're speaking to. It makes it more believable. If it isn't done that way, you might just as well stand in front of a podium and recite your lines. Interaction, interaction, interaction. That's the key."

"Carol, suppose you begin when Larry stops looking at his feet during the instruction and surprisingly tells you he's interested in a relationship."

"I haven't got that part memorized yet."

"Well, if you've read it, try acting the part and not just the same wording as the script. If you basically know what's taking place, it will come natural. The longer the play goes on, you'll find the script will seem generic, and your familiarity with the lines and scenes will melt into what the audience will recognize as talent. Now begin your lines. Larry, take your position. While dancing with her, pause, then present your lines. Carol, take it from there."

After presenting my lines, Carol paused, then looked up at me saying her line. "I don't think I should get into a relationship with a married man, do you?"

"OK, Larry, continue." Cheryl said.

"Well, if I wasn't married would it make a difference?"

Carol began dancing again as if she didn't want to answer.

"That's good. That's perfect. OK Larry, stop, then kiss her!" Cheryl said.

Carol pulled back slightly, then stopped.

"What's wrong, Carol? You're supposed to kiss him then see the gardener trimming the hedge outside the window. He just caught you kissing Larry. What would you do?" Cheryl asked.

"Let me try again." Roselyn said.

This time, she put a surprised expression on her face as if she were just caught by the gardener trimming a hedge outside the window. She broke from dancing and walked across the room to turn off the record player. I continuing my lines, "Could I possibly see you on the weekend? Sylvia is supposed to go with her brother to their parent's home. It's in New England. If you feel uncomfortable coming here since we've been seen by the gardener, we could meet for dinner somewhere away from here."

Roselyn continuing her lines, "OK, if I agree, let's not be demanding after dinner."

"I promise. I'll sit on my hands, so you can feel comfortable."

Cheryl said, "That's good! That's good!"

A round of applause came from Jan sitting in the audience, and a second round of applause came from the shadows in the rear of the theatre.

Coming into the light, Peter continued toward Cheryl. "Good morning!" He looked at his watch. "Rather, good afternoon. That scene looked very convincing, Roselyn."

Cheryl remarked, "When you're in the theatre, the biggest mistake is to call someone by their right name during the play. It will leave the audience completely baffled. Here, we'll always refer to the names of the people we're portraying."

Peter replied, "Then I take it I should be called Tony while I'm here?"

"Yes, I think you should."

Roselyn and I looked at each other again. It seemed Peter's attempt to sabotage the other two applicants for the play was successful, and last night was probably when it happened. Before we realized, it was already 1 p.m.

"Cheryl, I think it's about lunch time. Roselyn, would you care to join me?" I asked.

"I'd love to. We can discuss what we've learned this morning."

Looking at her watch Cheryl replied, "I think you're right. Do you want to call it a day, or do you want to come back?"

"Whatever everyone else wants to do is fine with me." I replied.

Peter, who wasn't invited, immediately asked Cheryl, "Would you care to join us?"

Looking as though she expected a private lunch with Peter, declined the group luncheon. Peter, noticing the disgruntled look she gave him, recanted his words by saying, "Cheryl, you said you would help me with my lines."

"Peter, if you're going to lunch with them, I'll see you back here later if you want to practice your lines. I'll be here all afternoon."

Jan quickly added, "I'll be here too."

The look on Peter's face told us as we expected. Cheryl's influence had everything to do with him getting the part, and it wasn't as yet cast in stone.

The conversation at lunch was about the parts we were given.

"Peter, you mentioned at the dinner table the other night there wasn't a part for a person my age. Why did you say that when you knew it wasn't true?"

He hesitated to answer, but looked at Roselyn instead, hoping for some help with his lie. She didn't speak, but gave him a look as if to say, "Oh well, now what are you going to do." It was obvious he didn't expect her to be silent and seemed very annoyed by it.

"We better be heading back to rehearsal," I said. "I want to get as much time in as possible. Cheryl has been helpful all morning, and maybe we can pick up a few more pointers."

Returning to the theatre, we rehearsed until late afternoon.

As we were wrapping it up for the day, Jan asked, "Peter, have you made up your mind to cut your hair and dye it black?"

"Yes, I'll see to it tomorrow."

"Well, I can't see to the cutting, but I can do the dying for you."

He seemed apprehensive to answer, looking at Cheryl he replied, "That's OK. I think I can get it done elsewhere."

Cheryl looked up from the script with an approving smile. "Well, tomorrow's Saturday. Is anyone interested in coming back for rehearsal?"

Roselyn quickly replied, "Yes, I am. Allen, will you?"

"Yes, the more I practice, the more comfortable I'll feel when the play opens."

Peter quickly said, "I think I'll join you."

Again, Cheryl gave him a look of disapproval, and he caught her expression.

"On second thought, I guess I shouldn't," Peter said.

Cheryl's attitude once again, immediately turned positive. As we left the theatre, Roselyn asked, "Cheryl, when is the play opening?"

"In about two weeks."

Jan quickly added, "The props will be completed and delivered to the theatre by the end of next week. That's when Florence will steam roll getting it all together. She wants to open before Thanksgiving weekend."

I replied, "Steam roll. That sounds ominous."

"Not really. Florence gets into it and gives her best. She never feels comfortable until the critics give their review, and the bugs are worked out of the play."

Roselyn replied, "Well, I guess we can look forward to a heavy rehearsal for the next few weeks."

"Yes, you can." Cheryl replied.

Returning to the house, the smell of Ethel's cooking reminded our stomachs they were hungry.

"Smells good," I said. "Roselyn, I'll see you at dinner." Going up the stairs Peter replied, "Not me, I have another dinner appointment."

Entering his room, he closed the door.

We were seated at the table as he entered the dining room to excuse himself for the evening, "Well, goodnight all. Roselyn, I'll see you in the morning for rehearsal," Peter said. He left the house, and I don't think anyone minded his absence.

Mrs. Green remarked, "Roselyn, Allen, we'll be leaving tomorrow morning. Would you mind if I give you my home address? I'd like to know how you make out with your careers."

Simultaneously, we replied, "I don't mind Mrs. Green." Then we laughed. The way she said it was as if she were already confirming our success.

***

The butler's part, David Canady, was given to a man by the name of Carl Dunn. He was 6' tall, very slim and quite handsome for a man in his early 40s. With graying hair at the temples, it made him look distinguished.

The Detective role of Bill Sloss was given to a man named Frank Ruff. He was around 5' 10", in his early 40s, balding and on the portly side.

Carl, who was playing the part of the butler, had some stage experience, but Frank had none. At this late stage of the game getting a cast together, Florence realized Frank would be somewhat of a challenge.

***

The next two weeks were a grind with long hours and constant coaching from Florence, with some assistance from Cheryl. The stage props were in, and it seemed to make a big difference with rehearsal. Instead of an imaginary scene, it gave us a dimension so as to speak, where we had boundaries.

In those two weeks we saw less and less of Peter at the boarding house, and a few nights he never made it home at all. At the theatre, it was obvious there was some sort of relationship between Cheryl and him, but it was never brought up.

On occasion, Jan seemed to be annoyed when Cheryl and Peter were in private conversation, but I never knew why.

Opening night finally arrived, and everyone was at the theatre early, smoothing over last-minute weaknesses with our individual parts. Looking out from behind the stage curtain, I got a lump in my throat seeing the seats being rapidly filled. I purposely missed dinner, not wanting to visit it twice by being nervous.

Roselyn approached me. "I missed dinner tonight. Maybe if we're not a complete flop, after the show we could go out somewhere for a bite?"

"I know. I missed dinner too. That sounds like a plan. Did you notice Peter seemed like he's been drinking?"

"Yes, I noticed. He seems to be drinking every day since we've auditioned. Maybe it relaxes him?"

"I hope it isn't due to your rejection. Not to be spying, but several weeks ago when he came in drunk the night before he got the part, I heard him ask what you were going to do if he didn't get his. That's when I heard you say there was no personal attachment and would probably never be," pausing to look out from behind the curtain at the audience again I continued, "I think that's what's bothering him."

"Well, I can't dwell on Peter's problems. Right now, I have my own. I can't seem to get the part right where I'm accused of trying to steal you away from your wife. I practiced it all wrong until I found the mistake, but it seems to be getting mixed up with the way I really want it to turn out."

"Don't worry. I'm sure you'll be fine. I have some of the same issues. Remember, this is only opening night."

Just then, Peter came over to join our conversation in somewhat an inebriated state, "Well, the night's finally here. Good luck!"

Roselyn remarked, "Are you alright to do your part?"

Confirming our suspicions, he said, "Yes, Cheryl's drummed it into me for the last several weeks."

At that moment, Jan came over to us. "I just want to check to see if everyone's comfortable in the clothes I selected."

Peter replied, "I don't. Not really. I'd rather have my hair blond and long again. These clothes seem strange to me when I look in the mirror. I sometimes feel like I'm two different people."

"Well, actually you are, maybe even three different people. The real you whcn you first camc for thc audition. Thc Tony Cappolla you're about to bring to life, and the Peter who suddenly acts different when you're talking to Cheryl, when I come into your company."

Roselyn and I suspected a little tension for the last week and a half as we were rehearsing, but put it aside thinking it was the long hours. It was becoming obvious that there was a three-way infatuation- or for the lack of proof, at least a closer relationship between them.

With everyone in position, the curtain opened to a packed house. It seemed like the fears of failure were dispelled with the opening lines from Cheryl. Her prior experiences in plays gave everyone the confidence they needed reciting their lines.

I dreaded to think, that without having her confidence, the audience could have paid good money to observe statues on the stage looking at one another for two hours.

Florence stood on the side-lines behind the curtain, prompting us, flailing her arms frenetically, where she suspected we may have difficulty with our lines. With script in hand, she paged through it as the play went on, miming our movements. Within the first half hour, she realized we weren't going to be a complete failure and became a little more settled.

Peeking from behind the curtain at the audience's silence, she realized their silence was due to them being transfixed on the play, which was a good sign. Other than the few times when there was a funny line, it seemed to be holding their undivided attention.

The curtain came down on the first half, and we anxiously went to the side-line to hear Florence's critique, and her lack of criticism was encouraging.

"Tony, you're supposed to be a suspect in murdering Sharon. The perfect defense- in fact, your only defense- is saying you were having consensual sex and during it, accidently smothered her. Try not to overdo your part acting as though it was a planned malicious attack. Other than that, I think everyone's doing well. Remember, this is only your first night, and looking out at the audience, so far, they seem to be enjoying the play.

At that moment, Mr. Cohen, the critic, came behind the curtain.

Florence asked, "Well, Charles, what's your opinion?"

"So far, it's holding the audience's interest. I haven't heard any grumblings after any of the scenes, but I'll know better at the conclusion if it's a success. I better get back to my seat."

The curtain rose on the final hour, and everyone seemed to be more confident with their roles. The last scene when Tony is confronted with being arrested for the crime brought the play to an end. The curtain closed and after we lined up on stage, it was reopened. There was no standing ovation, but there weren't missiles of vegetables being tossed either. It seemed like a mixed reaction.

As the players were named individually, we stepped forward to receive our accolades. For the butler David Canady, played by Carl Dunn, there was a mild round of applause.

Sylvia Cranston, played by Cheryl Freeman, brought a louder and somewhat sustained round of applause.

Larry Cranston, played by myself, brought another mild round of applause.

The gardener, a lesser role, played by Wally Williams, brought the loudest round of applause than myself or the butler. I think it may have been because of his appearance. Jan did a superb job with his dress, fitting his character to a T.

The maid, Jennifer Grimes, played by Sharon Fox, brought an equal amount of success.

And finally the detective, Bill Sloss, played by Frank Ruff, was about the same.

The curtain came down again to our relief, and we gathered to talk about the play's success.

After 15 minutes, Roselyn asked, "Well, Allen, are we ready to eat? I'm famished."

"Yes, I think so."

Chapter 4

As we were about to walk away, Jan announced, "You can leave your wardrobe in the costume department on your way out."

Being in normal dress just finishing the play, we had forgotten we were still wearing theatre property. Peter was the only one who remarked, "How could I forget? I'm anxious to get back in my jeans and sweater."

I was surprised when he didn't seem to mind when Roselyn asked about dinner. Was he giving up on the idea of having a relationship with her? Only being three weeks since her bold rejection, it was too early to tell.

After changing, I was in the hall outside wardrobe when I heard Jan ask Peter, "So you're leaving the bed and breakfast to move in with Cheryl?"

I paused, not wanting to barge in on their private conversation. I waited till there was nothing being said before knocking. Jan opened the door as if she were alone. She took the suit I was wearing for the play and thanked me. As she was hanging it back on the rack, I could see feet behind another section of costumes. It had to have been Peter, but why did he feel he had to hide?

"Goodnight, Jan."

"Goodnight, Allen."

I met Roselyn waiting at the back of the theatre by the exit.

"Are you ready to have that dinner?"

"If you don't mind, I'd just as soon settle for a light meal. A sandwich would be fine."

"Sandwich it is then!"

A bar called the Rathskeller was an establishment with a large fireplace on one wall, which took the chill from us a few minutes after being seated in front of it. Looking around, I noticed Carl and Cheryl sitting at a table in a darkened corner. They couldn't have possibly missed our entrance, the only way to that section of the bar, is down a set of open stairs. Realizing they'd been seen, Carl came to our table.

"Hello Carl, did you miss dinner too?" I asked.

"Cheryl and I were just having a sandwich discussing the success of the play. Would you care to join us?"

Roselyn quickly replied, "No, I think I've had enough discussion of the play for one night."

Returning to where he was sitting, we could see them talking for a few minutes then leave their table. As they passed, they said goodnight.

Our conversation was light, tending to shy away from the theatre. I asked, "So, are you going to continue at Mrs. Devlin's?"

"For the time being, I am. She made a special arrangement for what she'll charge me if I choose to stay. I think comparing that with paying rent for an apartment, furnishing it and all the rest that goes with renting, it sounded like a good deal. Besides, I enjoy her cooking. It's better than mine. How about you?"

"I was thinking along the same lines. She told me the same thing."

"Well, I guess we'll be in each other's company for more than just work. I'm looking forward to it."

The ending phrase was somewhat a surprise, but I was happy she said it; it sounded encouraging. After finishing our sandwich, we left for the boarding house.

Upon arriving, Mrs. Devlin greeted us enthusiastically. "Well, how did the play go? Was it a success?"

"No, Mrs. Devlin and you won't have to visit the produce section of the grocery store for the next week. We picked up all the vegetables that were tossed."

Standing back, she saw Roselyn laugh and realized I was joking.

"No, I'm only kidding. It went well. I think you'll have a few boarders for awhile. Roselyn and I decided we'll stay here."

"That's fine, that's fine. Peter came by about an hour ago and told me he was leaving in the morning, and went out again. He must have found an apartment. Roselyn, you saying you're going to stay is somewhat of a surprise. I assumed you were going to leave too."

"Peter never mentioned it to me," Roselyn said.

"Allen, would you rather move down to his room after he leaves?"

"No, Mrs. Devlin, I've become accustomed to my room. I think I'll stay there."

"Well, goodnight you two, I wouldn't have been able to sleep until I knew how successful you were."

I followed Roselyn to her room, and she stopped abruptly outside her door.

"Allen, I meant what I said when I told you I was looking forward to us working together."

"Me too!" Smiling, I walked past her to my room.

***

In the morning we were seated around the breakfast table when Peter came in. He announced, "Roselyn, I guess Mrs. Devlin told you I was leaving?"

"Yes, Peter, she did last night. Did you find an apartment?"

Ignoring her question, he went to his room and packed his belongings. Before we were through breakfast, he was back in the dining room.

"Roselyn, I'll see you later at the theatre. You too, Allen."

After making his exit, I asked, "Roselyn, would you care to take a walk by the river? With all the rehearsing, I've been neglectful with exercising."

"That sounds like a good idea. Wait, I'll get my coat."

Walking toward the river, we were surprised to see Cheryl drive by with Peter.

I remarked to Roselyn, "Before I turned in my suit to Jan last night, I heard her and Peter talking in the wardrobe room. When she answered the door, I saw someone's feet behind the costume rack. By the voice, I knew it had to be Peter. Why did he think he had to hide?"

"That's strange. One night last week, I saw him sneak her up to his room."

"Doesn't she have an apartment?" I asked.

"I don't think so. I think she still lives at home with her parents. From what she told me, they don't live that far away. I think they may be wealthy. She spoke about a butler at their home."

"Well, maybe him and Cheryl decided to get an apartment together."

R.J. Bonett

"Seeing him with Jan last night, and from what you just told me about him sneaking her up to his room, I just assumed that it would be Jan. I thought the way he got the part as Tony was through Cheryl."

"I thought that too. I guess we were both right."

I comically added, "We'll have to get Detective Sloss to investigate."

Roselyn laughed as we continued on our walk.

The leaves on the ground were crunching under our feet as we walked, and like a kid she began stepping on them.

She said playfully, "I remember as a kid we used to try stepping on the big ones. They make the most noise."

When she said it, something caught my eye. Whether it was the sun shining on her long auburn hair, giving it a reddish tint, or just the moment itself reflecting back on her childhood, I didn't immediately know. But I felt as though it was a spark I needed to take my mind off our work, and possibly toward a relationship.

I thought, 'Would she agree? I don't want to appear too aggressive. Maybe it's been so long since I was last involved that it's just my imagination of wanting to renew a relationship."

Trying to land a position with a theatre troupe had taken most of my time. In fact, it was probably the reason my wife of three years divorced me. I opted not to say anything, as we continued our walk.

Before we knew it, we were on Main Street looking in shop windows. As we passed the coffee shop, we saw Jan and Carl seated at the window. They appeared to turn away from looking at the street, but realized we saw them. Through the window, we could see Jan say a few words to Carl, then tap on the window to get our attention. She waved for us to join them and I looked at Roselyn and asked,

"Well, shall we?"

Roselyn hesitated. "If you really want to, I don't mind."

"Am I wrong? But if you were alone, I don't think you'd want to."

Looking at me with a grin, she said, "You're right, I wouldn't. But I didn't want to make the decision for both of us."

Realizing it was a very unselfish thought, I smiled. "Well then, we won't stay for coffee. We'll only say hello."

30

She seemed pleased with that, and we went inside.

"Hello! Jan, Carl. The coffee's pretty good here isn't it?"

"Yes, it is. Jan and I have been here before. Are you staying for some?" Carl asked.

"No, we were just going back to our rooms to get ready for rehearsal."

"We were just about ready to leave too."

Walking out the door, Jan asked, "Have you seen Peter this morning?"

Looking at each other, we wondered whether to answer in the affirmative.

Without elaborating, Roselyn tactfully replied, "We saw him briefly at the house this morning."

Carl remarked, "We'll see you later at the theatre."

Walking back to Mrs. Devlin's, we both had questions in our minds about Peter's relationships with Cheryl and Jan. Handsome enough to attract the attention of both women, it wouldn't be unbelievable for Florence Stark, the director, to also have a late age youth relationship. Arriving, we met Peter as he was exiting the house.

"I thought you were already gone?" Roselyn said.

"I just wanted to get a few things I left behind and thank Mrs. Devlin for the stay."

"We saw you drive by with Cheryl this morning. Are you moving in with her?"

"For now yes. She offered to share her pad with me. She has a really cool place overlooking the river. It was an old mill converted to apartments and a restaurant. Really nice!"

Roselyn remarked, "Well, we ran into Jan this morning. She asked whether or not we saw you. If she asks again, should I say anything about you and Cheryl living together?"

"No, I'll tell her. I made up my mind the other day when it was offered, but I haven't had a chance to be alone with Jan to let her know."

Roselyn quickly looked at me, remembering what I told her about him being with her in the costume room. I realized he was lying again, but why?"

"Well, we'll see you later at the theatre."

"Yes, I have to run. Cheryl's parked down the block waiting for me." Peter quickly walked down the sidewalk to her waiting car.

"Roselyn, I think we better get to the theatre early," I said. "I'm sure Florence is eager to put our performance under scrutiny. I'm anxious to hear her analogy."

"The way you said that, I feel like a kid about to bring home a bad grade to a disappointed parent."

I replied, "I think if it was that bad, she would have said so last night. I thought we could walk to the theatre. Are you ready?"

"I just have to get a sweater from my room. The theatre is a little chilly. They keep the thermostat turned down when there's no audience."

"I'll be right here," I said.

After she got her sweater, we headed out the door. Walking down Main Street, we saw what looked like Jan's car drive by with a man sitting on the passenger side. It pulled off onto one of the side streets into a small parking lot.

"Roselyn, I think that was Jan's car."

"I know it was. I saw her, but I couldn't tell who the man was."

"Maybe it was Peter? He did say he wanted to tell her about moving in with Cheryl."

"I wonder if she's going to the theatre today."

"She's not really needed. Everyone knows what they'll be wearing."

"I guess you're right," Roselyn replied.

Getting to the theatre parking lot, we could see Florence's and Cheryl's car in their assigned spaces.

"I hope we're not late. We better hurry up."

Walking a little brisker, I threw open the stage door. Both Peter and Cheryl were already there.

"Roselyn, I wonder who was in the car with Jan?" I asked.

"That's a good question. Maybe it's someone she knows from the area. Cheryl did say she lives near here."

"Good morning you two," Florence said. You might just as well sit in on this conversation. We've been going over a few things that need cleaning up a bit."

Just then, Carl came from the men's room. Leaning towards Roselyn I said, "I guess that wasn't Carl in the car either. Peter's here and he's here too.

It has to be someone she knows from the area."

"Maybe, but let's hear what Florence has to say," Roselyn said.

"Well, did anyone read the review in the morning paper?" Florence asked.

Looking at each other being silent, Florence understood we hadn't.

"Well don't be alarmed, I've seen worse criticism."

Looking at one another, we were surprised at her remark.

"I'm only kidding. The review wasn't bad at all. It did point out that some of the new cast were a little canned with their lines, but that would be worked out as the play progresses. I know Mr. Cohen has probably read it, and that's the important thing. Are there any questions?"

After a brief pause, no one responded.

"If you want to rehearse a little more before this afternoon's performance, you're free to work with each other. Just remember, everyone should be here at 12. Curtain call is at 1."

We began to go over our lines, when Florence called Peter to the side. We couldn't hear what was being said, but whatever it was caused Peter to raise his voice. "I don't think I should be singled out. Cheryl said I did fine."

Embarrassed by his loud outburst, Florence looked at Cheryl as though she disapproved with her expressing judgment of Peter's performance. Florence didn't pursue the conversation any further promptly leaving the theatre.

For the next two hours, we rehearsed our lines.

I said, "I don't know about anyone else, but I'm not going to forego lunch. Anyone else want to go along?" I asked.

Roselyn replied, "I'll go."

Frank took a brown bag he had placed on one of the seats opening it. He obviously thought of possibly missing lunch by bringing his own. Edward did the same, and they sat in one of the rows eating while discussing current events in the sporting world. They seemed to have mastered anxiety with playing their parts as only an older person can, putting things in their proper perspective. For now, lunch was more important.

Carl asked, "Do you mind if I tag along?"

"No, I don't mind. Peter how about you and Cheryl?" I asked.

"I don't know if Cheryl wants to go, but I'd like to wait until Jan comes.

There's something important I want to speak to her about."

It was obvious Cheryl knew as well as we did the importance of what he had to tell Jan. As we were leaving the theatre, Jan's car pulled into the parking lot.

"Where's everyone going? Is this a walkout protest?" Jan asked humorously.

"Not really. We're going to lunch. Care to join us?" I asked.

"No, is Peter inside?"

Cheryl replied, "Yes, he said he wants to speak to you."

She went directly inside, and we continued to the luncheonette.

***

In about an hour, we returned to see Edward, the gardener, and Bill Sloss, the detective, already in their dress for the show. Going to the costume room to check out our garments, Roselyn and I noticed Jan's eyes were red, as if she'd been crying.

"Jan, are you alright?" Roselyn asked.

She sniffled. "Yes, I'm fine."

After Jan handed us our clothing, we retired to our different dressing rooms to prepare. Walking into the men's dressing room, I saw Peter standing there.

"Peter, I just saw Jan. It looks as though she's been crying." I said.

"I know. It seems like she had some idea we were going to be getting an apartment together. I told her I was moving in with Cheryl. I think it upset her," Peter said.

"If it's not too personal, why would she think that?"

"I don't know. I never gave her any indication we were going to do that. We were never intimate."

I thought, According to Roselyn, she saw you sneak her into your room, and it sure wasn't to discuss the clothes you wear for the play. "Well, I was just asking. She seems like a sweet kid. Actually, it's really none of my business."

Peter looked relieved that I wasn't going to probe any further.

Going out on stage, everyone took their positions and at 1 p.m, the curtain rose. Cheryl didn't have to prompt us, and with the confidence of having gone through it last evening, the play went on without any problems.

At the end of the play the curtain fell again, and we had a few hours until the 7:30 performance.

Carl approached Roselyn and me.

"Are you two going anywhere between performances?" Carl asked.

"Not unless Roselyn wants to go for coffee," I replied.

"I don't think so, Allen. I'd like to find a quiet spot and go over this part I'm still having problems with. I just can't seem to get it right" Roselyn said.

"Well, I'll see you after we get back. Are you ready, Carl?" I asked.

"I think I'll just stay here too. I might go over my part as well," Carl said.

"Suit yourself."

Roselyn headed for her quiet spot, and Carl bid me adieu.

Before leaving the theatre, Frank asked, "I heard you say you were going for coffee. Would you mind bringing a cup back for me and Ed?"

"Not at all! How would you like it, cream and sugar?"

Frank replied, "Just light on the cream for me, how about you Ed?"

"Make mine the same. It'll be less confusing."

Getting to the coffee shop I made the purchase and headed back.

Walking through the parking lot, I saw Jan getting out of a car. She leaned in the car window as if she was saying something to the driver, and after closing the door, the car pulled away. She looked around then hurried toward the theatre. I called to her, but without looking back she ignored me and entered the building.

I thought, "That's strange. I wonder why she ignored me."

Walking in the exit door, I gave Frank and Edward their coffee then headed in search of Roselyn's quiet spot. I bought her one, thinking she might like a cup to settle her nerves. Hearing me in the hall, she came from the women's changing room.

"Roselyn, I brought you a cup of coffee. I thought..."

Interrupting in a quiet voice, "Can I talk to you a moment in private outside?"

"Yes, what's wrong? You seem upset."

I quickly followed her to the exit, anxious to hear her problem.

"After you left, I found a spot where I could practice the weak spot in my lines. I thought you may have changed your mind about leaving, but when I turned around, Carl was standing there. It startled me at first, but after regaining my composure, I mentioned that he would have to find his own quiet spot to rehearse. He said he wasn't sure of some of his lines and asked my opinion. Being polite, I told him I had to rehearse my lines first, then, I'll be more than willing to listen," she hesitated looking down at the floor. I asked, "That can't be all there was. What made you upset?" I asked.

With confidence in telling me she continued, "He said he'd rather practice his lines after the performance tonight. When I told him I couldn't, he tried to be more persuasive. I tried ignoring any further attempts of his suggestion, but he became adamant. It seemed as though his personal pride was injured by my rejection. When I went to leave, he leaned against the wall with his arm blocking my path. I told him he'd have to excuse me, and when I maneuvered around his arm, he gave me a look that sent a chill up my spine."

Looking at the exit door, I wondered whether or not I should re-enter the theatre and confront him.

"Did he ever make any attempts to see you on a personal level?" I asked.

"He made a few comments, but I never gave him any idea that our relationship was anything outside of the play. If he thinks it is, it's strictly something he's conjured up in his own mind."

"If you want, I'll speak to him after the performance tonight."

"Okay, but don't tell him I was frightened. Just let him know we're an item and let it go at that," Roselyn said.

"Should I build up my hopes, or are you just using me as an excuse?"

She smiled, and I took it to be a positive sign.

Re-entering the theatre, I went to the costume room to draw my suit for the play.

"Jan, I saw you getting out of a car on the parking lot and called to you but you didn't answer," I said.

"I guess I had something on my mind," she replied.

"Who's car was that?"

Avoiding eye contact she said, "Just a friend."

I made no more of it, and went to the dressing room. Carl was just finishing getting dressed as I walked in.

"Carl, Roselyn and I are an item. She tells me you made unwanted advances to her, and would appreciate it, if you wouldn't do it again."

Looking startled at my statement, he continued to the door. Before walking out, he turned toward me. "I didn't know that. Tell her I apologize," he said.

"I think you better apologize yourself. I think she'd like that," I suggested.

"First chance I get," he said.

Before the curtain went up, I saw him standing with Roselyn and assumed he was apologizing. After he walked away, I approached, and before I could ask, she thanked me.

"Then everything's OK?"

"Yes, he apologized. Thank you."

"Does that mean my role in this is over?"

"Not unless you want it to be."

"That's encouraging, how about a bite to eat after the performance?"

"It's a date. We better take our positions, the curtain's about to go up."

Whether it was a good feeling about the prospect of a relationship or familiarity of doing the play several times, I didn't know. The performance took shape just as Cheryl said it would and ended without difficulty. The audience response after we lined up before them, told us we were beginning to impress with our performances. As our individual names were called, we stepped forward. All of us received a round of applause and again, Wally the gardener received the loudest response. His simple home-spun demeanor with some of his interactions with the other players was eye catching.

After the curtain closed again, we all chided Wally about his popularity.

I said, "Wally, it'll be no time before you'll be doing plays on Broadway, or commercials on TV."

Cheryl agreed. "Nice job, Wally. You're beginning to get more accolades than me."

Heading for the dressing room, I said, "Roselyn, I'll meet you at the exit door of the parking lot."

"Fine, Allen. I'll only be a minute."

After she joined me at the exit, I held her coat as she slipped into it. Exiting, we saw Jan getting into the same gray Mercedes that dropped her off.

"Roselyn, do you know who's car that is?" I asked.

"I've seen it on the parking lot before. Why?" she replied.

"Just asking. I saw her getting out of it this evening before the performance. I called to her, but she ignored me and rushed into the theatre. When I asked about me calling to her, she blew me off, dismissing my question."

"I don't know, Allen, she seems to be troubled for a girl her age. Maybe she's having a hard time maturing. She does seem emotional at times. You said when you saw her in the dressing room she looked as though she'd been crying."

"That's right, but I thought it was only Peter telling her they weren't going to have a relationship. Maybe it's something else. I can talk to Peter. The next time we get together I'll ask."

Chapter 5

Across the Delaware River from New Hope is the small town of Lambertville, New Jersey. Like New Hope, it's been in existence for several centuries. On Main Street, Boar's Head Inn is a colonial landmark hotel and eatery and has been for several hundred years. The interior hasn't changed much in all that time, and the richness of the chestnut wood doors and wainscoting somehow adds to the feeling of being there during colonial times. An old book used for registering guests is prominently displayed in a glass case with the pages open to signatures of various famous people who had once visited.

Knowing Roselyn spent most of her time on the West Coast, I asked, "Have you been here before?"

"No, this is really neat. It feels like George Washington will come through the door any minute."

I added, "Or British and Hessian officers in full regalia with swords hanging at their side. Washington's Crossing is just down the road."

Laughing at the comment, we were ushered to a table close to the fireplace. The warmth of the crackling flames added to its charm, and I handed her a menu.

"What are you going to order?" I asked.

"Probably something light, just a small salad and coffee."

The waitress came to the table, took our order then promptly left.

I looked up as someone was entering the dining room. It was Jan, escorted by Charles Cohen, the critic and financier of the play.

"Roselyn: look who just came in."

Thinking they might want to join us, she waived her hand. Charles saw us near the fireplace, then spoke to the maitre d' who quickly escorted them to another area of the dining room.

"Roselyn, I wonder why they avoided us?"

"I know. He had to see me wave. I just don't know."

After our light meal and some small talk about likes and dislikes, we left. Going outside, we saw parked a few feet from the inn, a silver Mercedes.

"Roselyn, I think that's the same car I saw Jan getting out of earlier this evening, I wonder what the connection is?"

"Maybe they're discussing something about the costumes or an upcoming play."

I quickly added, "That doesn't sound encouraging."

"What do you mean by that?" she asked.

"If they're discussing another play; that means our employment is short-lived."

Smiling at me she said, "I didn't mean it that way."

Pulling up to the bed and breakfast, I leaned over and kissed her. She didn't reject my gesture and became very involved. It lasted about a minute, and I began to feel excited. It was arousing my hormones, and I knew we had to break it off.

"I think we should call it a night, don't you?" I said.

"Yes, I think so. We'll have to make an arrangement away from here. I don't think Mrs. Devlin would condone our behavior in her house."

"I'm sure she wouldn't."

Going around to her side of the car, I opened the door, and we went inside. Mrs. Devlin must have been in bed, and we quietly went up the stairs. Getting to Roselyn's room, we paused outside her door, and kissed again.

"Goodnight," I said.

"You too, Allen." She kissed her finger then put it to my lips.

It was beginning to feel good again, having a relationship with someone who seemed to care about me, a feeling I hadn't had for some time.

***

I awoke early and went for a short walk. When I returned to the house, Roselyn was coming down the stairs as I entered. The aroma of coffee and breakfast being made was welcomed.

"Good morning, Allen. You're an early bird today," she said.

New Hope

"I know. I only slept for a few hours, but it was so sound. It felt like I slept for 10. I think it's the best sleep I had since I've been here."

"I know that feeling. It's the most refreshing sleep you can have. Is that why you took a walk?"

"Yes, it's cool out, but with the sun shining, it's tolerable."

"I haven't been outside yet. Maybe after breakfast I'll go for a walk too."

"If you don't mind the company, I'll walk with you."

"I wouldn't mind."

The walk was enjoyable, and the more intimate conversation was reassuring of a relationship about to take place. Monday and Tuesday were off days at the theatre, and we agreed on a trip to Philadelphia for Monday.

Getting back to the theatre, we saw Jan. Roselyn thought it would be a perfect time to speak with her about Peter. Realizing I would only inhibit the conversation, I excused myself.

"Jan, I know you were upset the other day. Is it anything I can help you with?" Roselyn asked.

"Not really. Peter told me he was moving in with Cheryl. I had thought we were beginning a relationship, but I guess I was wrong."

"Jan, It's none of my business, but I know Peter probably better than you. He's the kind of person who feels superior to everyone and often says things that disregard a person's feelings. I'll give you an example. The first day he met Allen, he told him he should review the play he's trying to get a part in. He also told Allen there wasn't a part that fitted his age, which wasn't only a lie but insulting. When he says things, he often says them without thinking. If he misled you, it could be just his normal attitude."

"I suspected it when he had the conversation with Florence last week, when he raised his voice and she abruptly left the theatre. I think he might have been with her the night before. I'm sure, that's why he got the part in the play."

Roselyn replied, "I thought Cheryl might have been the reason he got the part."

"I thought so too, but I saw Cheryl later that evening, and she was with Charles."

"You mean Charles Cohen?"

41

"Yes, I think they must have had a relationship several years ago."

"What makes you think that?"

"Charles was a partner with my father in business. They had a falling out after Charles got his divorce. I think it may have been over the relationship he had with Cheryl. He was married to my father's cousin. It's only a suspicion. I really don't know for sure. At any rate, he's been like a mentor to me. I confide in him a lot."

"You live near here, don't you?"

"Yes, my father's house is a few miles south of here."

"Does he know that you're confiding with his former partner?"

"No, I didn't want to stir bad blood. I knew Charles was active with the theatre. That's why I asked him for a job. I realized after I began working here he was seeing Cheryl. I never mentioned it to my father because Charles gave me the job."

"Well, getting back to Peter, I wouldn't waste my time with a person like that. He'll only do what he has to do to get what he wants. If he has to use your feelings as a stepping stone, he'll do it. Of course, that's just a friendly piece of advice. You're not bound to take it."

"Thanks, Roselyn. That puts a different perspective on Peter. I guess I was just hoping for too much."

"One more question. After you got out of Charles car, Allen called to you and you ignored him rushing into the theatre. Why?"

"I was trying to hide the fact I was confiding in Charles. I didn't want Cheryl to know."

"I see. I'll mention it to Allen not to tell anyone."

"Thanks."

As Roselyn exited the dressing room, I asked. "How did the conversation go?"

"I enlightened her about Peter and his attitude. I think she'll be alright that way. She did tell me about her connection with Charles and would appreciate if you didn't mention her getting out of his car."

I made a gesture. "My lips are sealed. Well, two performances today and we're off to the big city."

She replied, "You sound excited."

"To dispel any illusions, yes, I am."

Within a few minutes, everyone took their respective places, and the play began. Whether it was the anticipation of Monday morning or lack of concentration, I didn't know, but I inadvertently said "Roselyn" instead of her character name Carol during the scene in the rec room. A flush look came over my face when I said it, and there was a slight murmur coming from the audience. Roselyn looked at me giving me a smile quietly saying, "Keep going. They may not have noticed."

It was a vain attempt at saving me from what Cheryl mentioned about baffling the audience with that kind of mistake. Being more mindful of what I was doing, the audience seemed to absorb the error, taking it in stride. At the end of the first half, Florence was waiting in the wings.

"Allen, what were you thinking about when you made that mistake?"

Looking at Roselyn, her face turned a light shade of red. Smiling, knowing the reason I said it, she quickly turned away.

"I guess I had something on my mind and wasn't thinking. It won't happen again."

"Good, now let's get ready for the last half," Florence said.

Before taking our positions, Roselyn approached me smiling and in a quietly devilish tone asked, "Allen, what did you have on your mind?"

Smiling, I said, "I guess our trip to the city."

"Well, we better not dwell on it. I almost made the same mistake," she added.

At the end of the first performance, we were leaving the theatre to have a bite to eat. Opening the exit door, we saw Jan getting into Charles car, then it quickly drive away.

I asked, "I wonder why they keep avoiding being seen together."

"She got into the intricacy of their conversation and how Jan confides in Charles a lot. She told me about the relationship with Cheryl a few years ago and Jan not wanting to start any trouble between them."

"If that's what she's worried about, it seems odd that they meet around the theatre."

"Well, actually it isn't. She does work here, and he's involved with the theatre."

Satisfied with the explanation, we continued to the restaurant. After eating, we discussed what time we would head to the city in the morning, then, went back to the theater for the second performance.

It seemed like the second performance went quicker than normal, and I made sure I didn't embarrass myself with the same mistake I made earlier. At the end of the performance, I handed my clothing to Jan, quietly telling her, "Roselyn explained to me why you didn't want it to get around about being with Charles. Your secret's safe with me."

As she looked over my garment placing it on a hanger she replied, "Thanks Allen."

Just then, something caught my eye. A closer look in the room, I saw someone standing behind a clothing rack, just as I had seen when she was talking to Peter. I only saw trouser legs and tan shoes, but I knew someone was definitely there. Why they felt they had to hide was something I didn't understand. Obviously for some reason, whoever it was, didn't want anyone to know they were there.

Pausing briefly, I added, "Jan, enjoy your two days off. Any special plans?"

"Not really, how about you?"

"Roselyn and I are headed to Philadelphia on our days off. She's never been there."

"That's nice. Have a good time," she said.

She seemed annoyed with my continued conversation and obviously didn't want to engage in more.

I repeated, "Well, enjoy your days off." Then I headed for the exit door to meet Roselyn.

Leaving the theatre, Roselyn commented, "Well, Allen, we got through another week and the attendance doesn't seem to be falling off. I guess if we had to use that as a measuring stick against our success, we won."

"I guess so." Then, in a loud voice, I proclaimed to an empty parking lot, "New York Theatre Guild, here we are."

We laughed, looking around, not realizing someone may have heard me.

Chapter 6

As the sky line of the city came into view, our mild conversation about likes and dislikes was pushed to the back of my mind. It was giving way to the anxious expectations of two days we would have together. Would they be intimate?

Exiting the expressway, I navigated the streets to the Bellevue Towers Hotel, a prominent landmark in center city Philadelphia. Entering the lobby, it was impressively dressed with holiday decorations as the rest of the city. Roselyn looked around after entering,

"I can see you're sparing no expense. Your expectations must be high."

"Whatever happens will happen. Whether I impress you with the luxury of where we stay really won't depend on me, it'll depend on you," I said.

She paused to look at me and said, "I don't think you'll have to worry about our days off being disappointing, but I would have just as well settled for a less expensive room."

Giving her a sheepish smile I asked, "Should I ask for two rooms or one?"

"I wouldn't want you to spend all your salary since the opening of the play. One room will be sufficient."

I smiled again. Could she read my mind as if I were an open book? Am I that obvious with my intent?

She took a seat in the lobby, while I registered at the reception desk.

The attendant asked, "How may I help you, sir?"

"I'd like a room for two."

"How many nights?"

"Tonight and tomorrow night. If you could possibly give us a room that has a view of the city, I'd appreciate it."

Looking at the far end of the desk then back at me, the attendant gave me the impression he was open for a gratuity for my request. Taking out my wallet, I retrieved a $20 bill. Folding it, I put it under my palm then slid it across the counter. Replacing my palm with his, he slid it off the counter and into his pocket.

"I think I can accommodate you. Now, let me see. I have a room on the sixth floor. It doesn't overlook the entire city, but I think you'll be more than pleased. Your face looks familiar. Have you stayed here before?"

"I'm from Philadelphia, but I've never had the pleasure."

"I'm certain I know your face from somewhere. Are you part of the theatre here?"

It was my chance to boast of my success, and I seized on the moment, mentioning having the part in the play in New Hope.

"I thought I recognized you. My girlfriend and I saw you in Murder at the Logan."

Feeling proud that he recognized me, I asked, "How did you enjoy the play?"

"I liked it. I think the gardener played a great role. The alcoholic brother to Sylvia was a little over dramatic. But all in all, it was very entertaining."

I completely forgot about Peter, with the anticipation of our days off and didn't comment. I thanked him for the accommodation then he rang for the bell boy.

"Take this gentleman and his companion to room 607."

Seeing the bell boy pick up our luggage, Roselyn joined us.

The attendant also recognized Roselyn and said, "She was in the play too. She was Carol Wilson."

"That's right," I said.

Roselyn remarked, "All this notoriety, I forgot my sunglasses to travel incognito."

I laughed. Then together we headed for the elevator.

Getting to the sixth floor, we entered our room, and I tipped the bell boy before he left. We looked out the window, and the view wasn't disappointing in the least. Just then, the phone rang. Answering it, it was the front desk.

"How do you like your accommodation?" he asked.

"Just fine. It's more than I expected. Thanks!" I said.

Looking around the room with approval, Roselyn took her bag to the bedroom to unpack.

She asked, "OK, we're here, now what?"

"I thought we could walk around the city and take in the sites, then have lunch wherever we find a spot that we like."

"That sounds good, but I'd like to freshen up before we head out."

"I'll wait for you in the lobby by the fireplace. It looks inviting."

"I'll see you in a little while," Roselyn said.

Returning to the lobby, I found a comfortable lounge chair and began to read the newspaper. Within 20 minutes, Roselyn joined me. She was wearing gray slacks with a bright red bulky knit sweater and a Christmassy silk scarf.

"I think you're wise to bring that scarf, but it may not be enough to keep your head warm if we're going to be outside for any length of time."

"I intend to buy a hat while I'm here."

With that, we headed out to explore the downtown area.

"You know Allen, being in California for the last several years, it almost made me forget about Christmas being cold, the way it was when I was growing up in Iowa. This seems more like Christmas."

"You mean the 'Currier and Ives' type of Christmas with the snow scenes?"

"Yes, that pretty much describes it to a T."

Walking on Market Street, we spied an upscale department store. After entering, we looked around and she saw a gray knitted hat on display.

Putting it on she asked, "What do you think?" Roselyn said, modeling it. "Should I buy it?"

"I think it's perfect with what you're wearing."

I knew the store every year at Christmas has a show of lights complimented with the narration of the Nutcracker. After watching the show, we sought a place to have lunch.

"OK Allen, since you're the tour guide, what's next?"

"There's a theatre here I could try and get tickets to."

Before I continued, she made a fist and pretended to hit me in the stomach.

"No thanks, no theatre. I'm not even going to think about it."

Walking Chestnut Street we window shopped, going in a few stores to get a look at what they had to offer. A vender on the corner was selling hot roasted chestnuts, and the odor was too tempting to resist.

"How about it, shall I get some?" I asked.

"OK, I haven't had them for years."

Totally enjoying each other's company we took in all the sites. The holiday cheer seemed to abound and seemed to be contagious with people scurrying about doing their shopping.

We stopped to watch the ice skaters displaying their talents at a local rink, each one trying to impress the less experienced with their movements.

"Roselyn, It's almost six o'clock. Where would you like to dine?"

"Anywhere you choose will be fine with me. Please, on my account, don't make it anywhere that's expensive."

"Fine, I know a quiet place that has great food and not too expensive. Do you like Italian food?"

"Yes, it's my favorite."

Cicero's an Italian eatery in South Philadelphia, has been there since 1920. The interior had polished dark wood with white tablecloths, and on each table was a wicker-based wine bottle with a candle. After being seated, the waiter lit the candle and handed us menus.

"Would the gentleman care to order a bottle of wine?" the waiter asked.

"Yes. Roselyn, what's your pleasure?" I asked.

"I'd like a merlot. How about you?"

"That sounds good. Waiter, make it merlot."

Looking around, she said, "This is such a neat little place."

"I know. I came here often."

After dinner we went back to the hotel, and as we walked through the lobby, I wondered what the rest of the evening would be like. Getting to our room, I noticed the bed was turned down with a piece of Andes mint on each pillow.

"Allen, it seems like they thought of everything."

"Yes, I can see that. Did you want to use the bathroom first?"

"If you don't mind," Roselyn said.

"No, go right ahead."

As I sat on the edge of the bed, I could hear the water running in the shower and felt a little awkward not knowing what to expect. In about 10 minutes, the bathroom door opened, and she waved for me to come to her.

"Allen, why don't you shower while I'm putting on my makeup?"

Taking off my clothes and putting on the bath robe from the hotel, I stepped in. She was standing at the vanity about to apply her makeup when I commented. "You don't need to put that on. You have a natural beauty."

Smiling she said, "OK, if you insist."

She stood there watching as I adjusted the water then disrobed, entering the shower. I could hear the bathroom door as she exited the room, thinking, "She's not at all inhibited with this encounter. I hope she won't be disappointed."

Finishing, I entered the bedroom to find her already under the blanket covered from the waist down. The lights had been adjusted to a soft atmosphere, and I could see her beautiful breasts.

"I hope you don't mind me being forward, I'm not wearing any underwear," she said.

"Not at all. In fact," I opened my robe revealing my naked body like an exhibitionist.

She laughed as I let the robe fall from my shoulders, sliding into bed beside her. I didn't have to worry about making a first move. She was aggressive. Rolling in and out of love, we enjoyed each other several times before falling asleep.

I opened my eyes to daylight coming through the window. I laid there examining her asleep for a few moments before she opened her eyes.

"I didn't wake you did I?" I asked.

"No, I've just been laying here wallowing in the comfort of a warm body next to me. If you don't mind, I'd like to take a shower."

"No, go right ahead. I didn't really want to get out of bed for awhile."

I watched as she walked naked to the bathroom. Her voluptuous figure and her forwardness was just what I needed. The experience that I thought would be awkward was anything but, and I was happy the relationship would flourish. Hearing the shower turned off, I entered the bathroom.

"You don't mind if I shower while you're putting on your makeup, do you?"

"No, go right ahead. I'm famished."

"Well, while I'm showering, why don't you order from room service?"

"What would you like?" she asked.

"Whatever you order will be fine with me."

As I was done in the bathroom, she was already dressed, sitting by the window.

"Look Allen! It's beginning to snow."

"I noticed. Aren't you glad you bought the hat?"

"Yes, this is our last day. I want to enjoy it as much as possible."

Just then, there was a knock at the door. Our breakfast arrived, and the steward placed it on the table next to the window. There seemed to be a few extras on the tray, and I inquired.

"There seems to be more here than I ordered."

"Yes there is," he replied, "Look at the card pinned to the flowers."

Picking up the card it read, "Enjoy, compliments of the hotel."

Before he exited the room, I gave him a generous tip and said, "Thank you, and whoever is responsible for this."

"That was really nice of him. Now, what are we going to do today?"

"Are you into art? If you are, Philadelphia has a great museum."

"That sounds good," she said.

After finishing breakfast, we put on our coats then left the room. Walking through the lobby, I stopped at the front desk thanking the manager for the free breakfast. He responded in kind with a nod and said, "You're welcome."

Walking outside, there was a dusting of snow on the ground and a light snow falling. Flagging a cab, we set out for the art museum.

Roselyn was impressed with the majestic Grecian-style building sitting atop the five levels of stairs, wide enough to accommodate a dozen people walking comfortably abreast.

"This is magnificent. It makes me feel as though we should be dressed in togas watching chariots go by," Roselyn said.

"Yes, it's one of the finest art museums in the country."

After taking in the fabulous collection for a few hours, I asked, "Where to from here?"

Hesitating, she said, "I was thinking about a quick lunch and then heading for some quiet time back at the hotel."

"Sounds good to me. This is the last day."

After lunch, we returned to the room and made love for the rest of the afternoon. We fell asleep and when we woke, daylight was fading. I looked at my watch and it was already 5 o'clock.

"Do you want to freshen up first?" I asked.

"Definitely, I'll only be a short time. You can shower while I'm putting on my makeup, I'm famished."

After making ourselves ready, we headed for another restaurant I was familiar with. After dinner we decided to take in a little more window shopping, then returned to the room. To my surprise, she was anxious to return to love making.

I thought, "I don't know whether she's only trying to fulfill a thirst before going back to the boarding house, or whether she's trying to satisfy an insatiable urge, but I'm determined to fulfill whatever it is."

The hesitancy of getting out of a warm bed was compounded by the total satisfaction of a weekend that far exceeded my expectations. Looking at Roselyn asleep, I decided to go first into the bathroom. Taking a shower was like bringing me back to reality. In a few hours, we'll be heading back to New Hope.

While in the shower, Roselyn entered the room.

Opening the shower door, she asked, "Is there any room for me?"

Taking her by the hand, I helped her step in saying, "I think so."

I lathered up the soap with my hands and began running them over her smooth skin. Looking up at my face, she said, "Now it's my turn."

I quickly became aroused as she ran her soapy hands over every part of me. My body reaction was as if it was our first time.

"You know this is dangerous. Checkout time is in one hour," she said.

"I know. Maybe we shouldn't start," I replied.

With a smile she replied, "I didn't mean that we shouldn't, I just said that to make you aware of the time."

Exiting the shower, we quickly dried each other then headed for the bed. After making love once more, it was a mad scramble to freshen up and pack our bags.

Before exiting the room, I looked to make sure we didn't leave anything before turning out the light and closing the door.

Getting to the lobby, we were greeted by the clerk who checked us in.

"How was your stay?"

Commenting simultaneously as Roselyn and I looked at each other, "It was great!"

Roselyn and I smiled then asked, "Is the hotel still serving breakfast?"

"Yes. Here, let me give you a complimentary card."

"Thanks, thanks a lot," I said.

After breakfast we packed the car and headed north. Watching the city fade through the rear view mirror was like coming out of a dream you didn't want to end. She drew close, which made me feel assured she was completely satisfied with our weekend, and I was relieved that she seemed to be looking forward to our relationship.

Chapter 1

Driving down Main Street in New Hope, there were more people than usual for a Wednesday due to Christmas shopping. Difficult to find a parking space, we continued to the boarding house. Going in, we were immediately confronted by Ethel.

"How was your trip to the city?"

Roselyn replied, "It was great. Allen sure knows his way around."

"Not to alarm you, but a detective was here while you were away," Ethel said.

I said jokingly, "Was it Bill Sloss?"

Ethel, not being familiar with the name, looked a little confused. "No, I wrote his name down. It's on my desk."

Realizing it was more serious than expected, we hastily followed to her office.

"Here it is. His name was Mike Taylor. He asked if I ever saw a girl by the name of, now let me see. I know I wrote that down too. It's difficult to remember when you're my age."

Looking at the paper, she said, "Here it is. Her name was Jan, Jan Dougherty. He wanted to know if I ever saw a girl here by that name. I told him I didn't, but mentioned maybe one of you know her. I told him you would be back on Wednesday, and he asked if you would call him at this number."

Roselyn and I looked at each other. Roselyn knew Peter had Jan in his room last month, but didn't tell Ethel.

"Did he say what it was about?" I asked.

"No, he just asked if I could relay the message to you."

Taking the note, I said, Mrs. Devlin, would you mind if I use your phone?"

"No, go right ahead, I'll close the door so you can have some privacy."

"Thank you."

After closing the door, I looked at the paper and said, "Roselyn, I wonder what this is about?"

"We'll soon find out. Give him a call."

After dialing the number, a voice on the other end announced, "Taylor detective agency, Detective Mike Taylor speaking. How can I help you?"

I immediately realized it wasn't the police, and felt a little relieved.

"My name's Allen Simpson. I live at Ethel Devlin's Boarding House on Canal Street. She tells me you came here inquiring about Jan Dougherty. Is there something I can help you with?"

"I just wanted to know if you or Roselyn Carter ever saw her at Mrs. Devlin's."

"I know I haven't, but just a minute. Roselyn's right here. I'll ask."

Holding the phone to my chest, I motioned to Roselyn. "How should I answer his question?"

With a shrug of her shoulders, it told me she didn't want to reveal what she saw. In a low tone, "Ask him again what this is all about?"

Thinking for a moment about how to answer I said, "Detective, Roselyn and I are in a play at the New Hope Theatre. Jan is set coordinator and costume supervisor there. What's this all about?"

"I've been hired by a person I'm not at liberty to divulge. Let's just say the person is interested in her associations outside the theatre."

"Should I mention this call to Jan when I see her for tonight's performance?"

"I would appreciate it if you didn't. In any case, you or Roselyn never saw her at the boarding house, is that correct?"

"Yes, that's correct."

After I hung up the phone, Roselyn anxiously asked, "Did he tell you what it's about?"

"No, not why he's making the inquiry. Just the fact that someone he wasn't at liberty to divulge, was interested in who she might be seeing."

"Well, we don't have much time to figure it out. We'll be late getting to the theatre."

Looking at my watch, I said, "You're right. I'll have to drive us there."

She replied, "I'll see you in a few minutes. I just want to get something from my room."

She returned to the front door with a bewildered look. "Allen, something's amiss here!"

"What's that?"

"Someone's been in my room while I was gone."

"Maybe it was Ethel checking to see whether your window was closed."

"I don't think so. Whoever it was lost an earring." She opened her hand to show me. "This isn't one of mine."

"Did Peter have a key to your room?"

"Not unless he made a copy from mine. That would be the only way he would have one. He gave his key back to Mrs. Devlin, and I never gave him mine."

"Well, maybe you should ask him."

"I will, the first chance I get."

We arrived at the theatre just as Peter was getting out of Jan's car. Before closing the door, he leaned in and kissed her.

"Roselyn, they seem to be still having an affair. Here's your chance to ask him about the key."

"I'll follow him in the theatre then ask."

"Do you want me to go with you?"

"No, I'd like this discussion to be between me and him."

"Okay, but if he gets to be a pain in the ass, let me know."

"I will!"

"I'll see you back stage before curtain call."

When I entered the dressing room, Peter was involved in a discussion with Carl and abruptly stopped at my entry.

He asked, "Allen, how was your weekend?"

"Fine, Roselyn and I went to the city for two days."

Looking up from tying his shoe he said, "Good, isn't she?"

I grabbed him by the collar, shoving him against the wall, "What the hell is that supposed to mean?"

"I'm sure he meant nothing by it other than exposing his hurt feelings,"

Carl said.

"Well, Peter, if you didn't act so high and mighty, maybe you could have been with her," I said.

"Let's not get to the point where we'll forget our lines," Carl said as he exited.

"You're right. By the way, Peter, did Roselyn ask you about having a key to her room?"

"Yeah, she said something about a key. I told her I didn't have one. That's how I knew you were together on your days off."

"Did she show you the earring she found on the floor? She said it didn't belong to her."

"Maybe Ethel lost it, or maybe it was something a previous renter lost."

"By looking at the earring, it wouldn't be something Ethel would wear, and for as long as Roselyn's been in that room, I don't think it would have gone unnoticed. I did remember seeing something similar on Jan a while back," I said.

"I told Roselyn I didn't have a key. Besides, how would I have gotten in without Ethel knowing it?"

"Don't play games with me, Peter. Roselyn saw you sneak Jan into your room one night when you were still rooming there."

Peter, giving a surprised look, nervously responded, "Was she checking on me?"

"Not really. She just happened to be opening her door when she saw you," I said as I exited the room.

Gathering back stage prior to curtain call, I said, "Roselyn, I just had a confrontation with Peter in the dressing room."

"What about?"

"First, it was a smart ass referral about you being good in bed."

"That bastard! He wouldn't know the first thing about that. He's never had the pleasure," she responded angrily.

"I knew that when I heard you telling him you weren't attached by an umbilical cord. I wasn't eavesdropping. I just happen to be passing your room when you told him."

"That still pisses me off that he would imply such a thing. I'll let him know where we stand the first opportunity I get."

"Just be careful. He seems like he's a little possessive."

"Well, you have to have something before you can be possessive. Like I said, he never had the pleasure. Curtain call, we better take our positions."

Leaving the theatre that evening, I asked, "Did you have a chance to speak with Peter?"

"Yes, I told him he had no right to say that. I wouldn't consider having an affair with the likes of him. I demeaned him, trying to hurt his feelings as much as I could. He'll regret the day he ever said that."

"I'm glad it's settled," I replied.

***

The play was becoming more successful as it went on, and every performance, except Christmas Eve, was a packed house. Christmas Day and the whole week prior to New Year, there were two performances daily, which made life miserable. There was only a brief encounter with Peter during that time, but it was amicable, and I think his hurt feelings past.

Roselyn and I met, returning our costumes to the dressing room on New Year's Eve. I asked, "Roselyn, how should we bring in the New Year?"

"I think everyone is getting together at the Lambertville Tavern. It sounds like it might be fun. Jan, are you coming?"

As Roselyn was handing Jan the garment she wore for the play, it accidently slipped from her hand.

"Sorry Jan."

"That's alright. They need to be sent out to be cleaned."

As she bent down, Roselyn tapped me on the arm, directing my attention to the back of Jan's neck. There were visible bruises she was trying to hide with the scarf she was wearing.

"Jan, you must be cold wearing that scarf?" I said.

Pulling the scarf tighter to her neck, she said, "It's always a little colder in the prop room."

"Well, if you're going, you can ride with us. Roselyn said I'm designated driver tonight."

"That's alright. I'll find my own way," Jan said.

At that moment, Carl came to the door. "Jan you can go with me if you'd like. I don't intend on staying long."

"Thanks, Carl. I think I might just take you up on that offer."

"Allen, I'd like to go by the house to wish Ethel a Happy New Year, and put on another blouse," Roselyn said.

"Your carriage is waiting, Cinderella," I replied.

Walking across the parking lot, Roselyn held tight to my arm. "Did you see the bruises on Jan's neck?"

"I certainly did. I know it's chilly in the theatre after the performance, but the scarf she was wearing had nothing to do with the temperature. That kid's hiding something. I hope she knows what she's doing going with Carl."

"I do too! Hey, you haven't given me a New Years Eve kiss yet."

"I'll take care of that as soon as we get in the car."

After a long kiss, the car finally began to warm.

"Roselyn, do you see that black van parked over there? It's the perfect cover for someone following a person. I wonder if it's detective Taylor? Isn't that Jan getting into that Mercedes? I thought she was going with Carl."

We watched as the Mercedes traveled about 20' then came to an abrupt stop. The passenger door opened and Jan stepped from the vehicle. With the door still open, she seemed to be having heated words with the driver.

Rolling down my window, we couldn't hear the entire conversation, but we did hear Jan say in a loud voice, "I'll see whoever I want. You're not my father."

After slamming the car door, she quickly returned to the theatre, and the Mercedes slowly pulled away.

"Look, the van's pulling away too. He must be following Charles. Maybe we should go back and see if there's anything we can do for her."

"I don't think she would want us to be involved. It may only embarrass her."

Getting to the boarding house, we wished Ethel a Happy New Year.

She responded in kind replying, "I've been waiting for you two. That's the only reason I'm still awake. If you don't mind, I'll say goodnight."

We watched as she slowly walked down the hall to her room near the kitchen.

"Allen, she's the sweetest thing. We're lucky to be here."

"I know, I was thinking the same thing."

After Roselyn changed blouses, we headed for the Lambertville Tavern.

While looking for a parking space, we saw Jan and Carl walking toward the building.

"Look, she came with Carl," Roselyn said.

"I see them."

After finding a parking space two blocks away on a side street, we walked arm and arm to the tavern. Rounding the corner I noticed a black van parked on Main Street near the entrance.

"That looks like the same van that was on the parking lot at the theatre," Roselyn said.

"I think it is, and that looks like the same silver Mercedes Jan got out of, Charles Cohen's."

"Well, if he's in the bar, that would mean he's not the one having her followed," Roselyn said.

"Not necessarily."

"Enough; with talking about everyone else's problems, Happy New Year!"

"You too," I said and gave her a light kiss.

Going into the lower level of the bar, I happened to look over her shoulder and saw Peter looking in our direction.

"Roselyn, Peter's looking over here. I never thought to ask, but did you have a chance to speak to him after your tongue lashing?"

"No, I think he tries to avoid me as much as possible."

It seemed like the whole cast was here and greeted our entrance with a boisterous, "Happy New Year!"

Finding two empty seats, we discovered they were being saved for us by Cheryl.

"Thanks for saving them," I said.

"My pleasure."

As I scanned the room, I saw Charles speaking with Florence. "Look, Roselyn, Charles is sitting over there in the corner talking to Florence."

Giving me a stern look as though I was about to be scolded, she said, "I thought we were going to forget everyone else's problems?"

Just then, the lights grew dim, giving me a reprieve from answering.

The announcement was made. "Happy New Year, everyone, the champagne being passed around is on the house."

Several people began to sing Auld Lange Syne, and before a complete sentence was finished, everyone had joined in the throng. We never made it past the first few lines opting for a kiss instead. After our lips parted, I opened my eyes to Peter standing next to our table looking at us.

"Well, Roselyn, don't I get a New Year's kiss too?" Peter asked.

"I don't think so."

After her reply, he quickly left the table with a look of rejection.

"I don't believe he had the nerve to ask you that question," I said.

"Well, I told you when you first came to Ethel's. He has a knack for turning people off with his thoughtless statements. That's what I call his California attitude."

"Do you want to leave, or do you want to stay for awhile?"

"If you don't mind, I'd like to go."

"Is it because of what he said?"

"No, I'm just tired. A few drinks always has that affect on me."

Leaving, we passed Charles, about to get in his car. I asked, "Leaving early, Charles?"

"Yes, I'm not one for the party atmosphere. Goodnight!"

As he pulled away, Roselyn pointed, and said, "Look, Allen, that black van's pulling away too. It has to be following Charles."

"I wonder why?" I asked.

"That's a good question," she replied.

After returning to Ethel's, we kissed goodnight, then retired to our rooms.

I was awoken during the night by what seemed to be a frantic knock at my door.

"Who is it?"

"Allen! Allen. It's me, Roselyn."

"Just a minute."

Looking at my alarm clock, it read 4:00 a.m. Hurrying to the door, I opened it to Ethel and Roselyn excitedly speaking at the same time.

"Whoa, whoa, One at a time. What's this all about?" I asked.

"There's a detective downstairs, he wants to speak to us."

"You mean the private detective?"

"No, this is a detective from the police department."

"I'll be down in a minute after I put on my shirt and shoes."

As I entered the parlor, Roselyn looked visibly upset.

"What is it, Roselyn?"

"I'm detective John Kadelack from the New Hope Police Department," he said.

You and Miss Carter here were at the Lambertville Tavern tonight with the rest of the theatre group, weren't you?"

He was a man in his early 40's thin, with gray hair and sharp facial features.

"Yes. Why? We all met there after the performance," I answered.

"Was Jan Dougherty there?"

"Yes, she was."

"Did you see her with anyone?"

"She went with Carl Dunn. He's one of the players."

"Did you see them leave together?"

"No, Roselyn and I left earlier than anyone else for the exception of the play's critic and financial backer, Charles Cohen. Why?"

Pausing for a few moments he said, "Jan's in the hospital. She's been beaten pretty bad."

Roselyn became physically and emotionally upset, asking, "Will she be alright?"

"Her injuries aren't life-threatening, but she's giving us a few conflicting stories as to what happened. First, she said she was grabbed outside the station by someone she didn't know. Then, she said it was while she was waiting for a ride to pick her up. I suspect she knows who did it, but refuses to tell us."

"Is there anything you can tell me about who she sees, or who she may have a relationship with?" the detective asked.

I replied, "I know she went with Carl Dunn, but I don't know if she left with him. I've seen her in the company of Peter and Carl several times, but I don't know any more than that about her personal life."

He asked, "How about you Miss Carter?"

"No, I don't know any more than that either. Who took her to the hospital?"

Looking at his note pad, he said, "Florence Stark. Do you know her?"

"Yes, she's the director of the play. Did she tell you what happened to her?"

"I just got her name from the receptionist at the hospital. She apparently didn't stay after dropping her off. I haven't spoken to her yet. Well, if that's all you can tell me, I'll say goodnight. If you remember anything that will be helpful, here's my number at the police station."

Escorting him to the front door, I said, "Goodnight officer!"

Roselyn asked, "Mrs. Devlin, could you by chance make a pot of coffee? Allen and I have a few things to discuss."

"Certainly! Excuse me for saying it, but this is a hell of a way to start the New Year! You can sit here in the kitchen and talk. I'm going back to bed."

After pouring the coffee, we sat down to rehash what had been said.

"I wonder how Florence wound up taking her to the hospital," Roselyn asked.

"I can't figure that out, crisscrossing between relationships. Unless Charles met her later, I doubt it could have been him. The van that was following him would have seen something. I wonder who she left with."

"We don't have to be at the theatre until 12. Maybe we should go to the hospital in the morning and see if she'll confide in us."

"That's just what I was thinking. We'll go after breakfast. Now, I'm going back to bed."

"Me too!"

Getting back to sleep was a monumental task, tossing and turning trying to piece this all together. Roselyn was right about one thing. Jan was involved in a relationship that proved to be dangerous.

I finally fell asleep and was awaken by the sun shining through the window.

When I got to the dining room, Roselyn was already finished with her breakfast.

"Good morning, did you get back to sleep?" Roselyn asked.

"I tossed and turned for the better part of an hour, but yes, I did."

Mrs. Devlin entered the room and said, "Allen, Roselyn already ate, would you like your breakfast now?"

"I think I'll just settle for toast and coffee. Roselyn and I want to visit Jan at the hospital," I replied.

"That was terrible. Is she a young girl?" Ethel asked.

"Yes, too young for a relationship that's dangerous," Roselyn replied.

Arriving at the hospital, we saw Florence and Cheryl coming down the hall.

Roselyn asked, "Florence. How is she?"

"She's bruised pretty badly, but nothing life threatening. She's still very upset," Florence said.

"The detective came to the boarding house last night and told us what happened. He asked if we saw her leave with anyone. We left before anyone else except Charles. He left just before we did. Were you there when she left?" I asked.

"Yes, she left by herself," Florence replied.

"The detective did tell us you brought her here. She told the detective she was waiting for a ride when it happened. He also said she gave several conflicting stories. I don't think they believe her. What did she tell you when you drove her here?" I asked.

"When I came outside, she was leaning on a parked car. I thought she was sick from drinking, but when I tapped her on the back, she looked up and I could see the blood coming from her lip and nose. She was crying hysterically and all I could think of was getting her to the hospital."

"Was Carl and Peter still there when you left?" I asked.

"I think so. There were quite a few people crowded in there so I didn't notice. Cheryl, did you see them?"

"I was talking to Peter, so I know he was there. I don't remember seeing Carl though," Cheryl said.

Roselyn and I looked at each other. "Well Roselyn, we better get in there to see her. Florence, we'll see you at the theatre," I said.

"Allen, you mentioned seeing someone standing behind a clothing rack at the prop room when Jan was there last night. Is there anything you can remember, something, maybe the color of the bottom of the trouser legs or the shoes?"

"I remember the shoes were an oxford brown, and I don't think anyone in the play is wearing that color shoe. The trouser legs, if I can remember were light gray."

"You said you heard Peter's voice before you went in."

"No, that was the first time when she was upset. The second time was the night before our trip to the city. I remember telling her about our trip, but she seemed to be annoyed with me continuing the conversation. That's when I saw the trousers and shoes I'm describing."

"Well, let's go in and see if she'll confide in us," Roselyn said.

The first glimpse at her told us she took a few heavy blows to the face. Her lip was stitched, and her left eye was blackened.

Lying there in a hospital gown with short sleeves, we could see bruise marks on her arms. Some of them were yellow, which indicated they were already well into the healing process, and didn't happen last night.

"Jan, what happened?" Roselyn asked.

Looking down at herself. "I'm a mess aren't I?"

"A detective came to our boarding house last night to ask a few questions. That's how we knew you were here. We wanted to see if we could help in any way."

"Not really, unless you can turn back the clock before last night."

"Jan, I know you've been having problems with some of the people from the troupe. Was it someone we know?" I asked.

Being taken off guard by my question, she quickly turned her face toward the window. It was obvious to Roselyn and me that I struck a nerve.

"Is it something with Peter?" I confided. "I know he was in the prop room last month standing behind the clothing rack, I heard you talking to him before I opened the door. I knew you were upset too, because you looked like you'd been crying. I don't know whether it's my place to say, but the detective doesn't think you're telling him the truth."

Roselyn asked, "Come on Jan, we're only trying to help. We heard you yelling at Charles when you got out of his car last night before going to the station.

We heard you say, 'You're not my father!' then rush back into the theatre. What was that all about?"

"Look, I'm glad you came to visit, but these are my problems, I'll work them out."

New Hope

"So it wasn't an unknown person that accosted you on the street while you were waiting for a ride," I asked.

Looking back at both of us, she didn't have to answer. It was someone she knew. Just then a man entered the room, looked at us then gave Jan a kiss on the cheek. Biting his lip in anguish at the sight of her, he said. "Jan, what happened?"

"Allen, Roselyn, this is my father, Sam Doherty."

He was a man in his mid 50s, well over six feet tall, and still had the frame of someone used to keeping in shape. Dressed in a blue suit, his reddish brown hair with a graying accent at the temples, made him look distinguished.

Extending my hand, I said, "Roselyn and I are part of the theatre troupe. We wanted to see how Jan was doing. We were about to leave."

Roselyn said, "Well, Jan, if you want to talk, you know how to reach us."

Halfway down the hall, Roselyn suddenly stopped.

"Allen, I forgot my gloves. I left them on the end cabinet in her room- I'll be right back."

I followed her back down the hall. We noticed the door to her room was closed. Pausing outside, we could hear Jan's father accusing Charles of being the one who did it and stopped to listen.

We could hear Mr. Doherty say, "Jan, I don't want to upset you, but I know you've been confiding in Charles. I don't know why you feel you have to talk to him instead of me. Aren't I as important to you?"

"It's not that, father. Since you've broken partnerships with Charles, he seems to be more interested in my future."

"You mean by getting you the job at the theatre?"

"Yes, and listening when I have personal problems. Since you've remarried, home just doesn't seem the same."

"Well, Victoria has never given you a reason to feel you weren't wanted, has she?"

"No, not at all. I don't know. It just seems different."

"If I find out it was Charles that did this to you, he's a dead man. I already owe him one for your aunt. She would have never committed suicide if it wasn't for him."

"Is that why you ended your partnership? I never knew that," Jan said.

"Yes, he's always had an eye for young girls, girls that are vulnerable like you who believe he has no other motive than your personal interest."

The conversation stopped briefly when Roselyn knocked.

"Excuse me, Jan, I left my gloves on the bedside cabinet. Here they are! Well, goodbye again."

Walking down the hall, we realized there seemed to be a deep-seated hatred for Charles by Jan's father, I wonder if he's the person having him followed?"

"According to the conversation, he certainly has cause to do so," she replied.

***

Returning to the theatre dressing room, I saw the male cast getting dressed for the performance.

Peter said, "Allen, you better hurry. It's almost curtain call."

"Roselyn and I just returned from the hospital. We wanted to see how Jan was doing."

Wally asked, "What's wrong with Jan? Is she sick?"

"No Wally, she was beat up last night after she left the bar."

"Beat up? Who in the world would do that to such a sweet kid?"

The surprised look on his face, as well as Peter's, told me they knew nothing about it. Carl kept dressing and didn't seem to have the same surprised reaction. Was it because he had already been told, or did he have personal knowledge about it?

"After the performance it would be a nice idea if you pay her a visit. I'm sure she would appreciate it."

Carl asked, "Did she have any idea who did it?"

"I think she knows. I think she just doesn't want to say."

Again, his question didn't seem to be as much as a concern. It sounded like a self-defensive statement.

Taking position behind the curtain, Roselyn asked, "Did you tell them what happened to Jan?"

"Yes, I did."

"What was their reaction?" she asked.

"Peter and Wally were surprised, but it didn't seem to have the same affect on Carl. I think he knows something about it."

"Well, we can visit her again between performances. Maybe she'll decide to tell us."

"I think all of us will be going," I replied.

The performance didn't seem to have the same gusto as all the previous performances, and during the break, Florence was vocal about the lack of enthusiasm on everyone's part.

When the curtain came down at the end of the performance, the audience's reaction was also less enthusiastic.

Roselyn said, "Does anyone need a ride to the hospital? You could ride with us after we change."

"I'd like to ride with you," Florence replied.

"How about you Cheryl?" Roselyn asked.

"I think Peter and I will go by ourselves."

"Carl, would you?" Roselyn asked.

"No, I think I'll wait until tomorrow. There's no sense all of us going at the same time."

Arriving at the hospital, we met Jan's father who was leaving. Roselyn said, "Florence, Cheryl, Peter, Wally, this is Jan's father, Sam Dougherty."

Looking at them he replied, "Glad to meet you, and thanks for the concern for Jan."

"How's she doing, Mr. Dougherty?" I asked.

"She's in better spirits. And please, call me Sam."

Entering the room, everyone expressed their condolences about what happened. Peter seemed to have the biggest concern, kissing then hugging her. Cheryl seemed perturbed when she saw Peter's reaction.

"Jan, I'm glad you're feeling better. I think I'll wait outside," Cheryl said.

"Thanks for coming!" Jan replied.

"Do you know the person that did this to you?" I asked.

Again, she hesitated, "No, Allen, I don't."

Cheryl never returned, and within a half hour, we were ready to leave. Outside the room I asked, "Peter, I think we've stayed long enough."

"No, I'm going back in. I want to stay a little longer. I'll take a cab home," he said.

I noticed Cheryl waiting by the front door and asked, "Peter, what about Cheryl?"

"I'm sure she'll understand," he replied.

Roselyn and I looked at each other with skepticism of his reply. Leaving the room, we encountered Cheryl, informing her about what Peter said.

Her reaction was as we thought-hostile to say the least. She shoved open the front door and left with a vengeance.

We were pulling into the parking lot at the theatre to drop Wally off when we saw Cheryl speeding out of the parking lot.

"I wonder what she's pissed off about?" Wally asked.

He didn't have any idea of the love triangle surrounding the cast, and we chose not to tell him.

After exiting the car, Roselyn asked, "Allen, I never suspected Peter to still have affection for Jan. That was a total surprise."

"Me either. How will this little display of affection affect Peter's relationship with Cheryl? I hope it doesn't spill over into the play. The performance this afternoon was terrible. It just didn't flow as it normally does."

"I know," she replied. "Florence looked a little pissed during the intermission. She realized it."

When we arrived home, Ethel asked, "How was the kid that was beaten up? When you didn't make it home for dinner, I imagined you paid her a visit at the hospital."

"Yes, we did. She seems to be coming along fine."

"Well, I got another phone call from Mike Taylor, that private detective. He asked if you'd call him when you come in. You can use my office while I warm your dinner."

"Thanks Ethel," Roselyn replied.

We wondered what he wanted this time and returned his call.

"Detective Taylor, this is Allen Simpson. You wanted to speak to me?"

"Yes, it's about Jan taking the beating."

"What did you want to know?"

"I was surveying the Lambertville Tavern when I saw Charles Cohen leave. I followed him to his home and saw a man confront him in his driveway. If you can tell me, what does he have to do with Jan?"

"As far as I know, he was a partner to Jan's father, and they had some sort of falling out."

"I rolled my window down when the confrontation looked like it was going to be physical," Taylor said. "The words were pretty heated, and I was prepared to blow my cover if necessary."

"If you're using a black van, Roselyn and I thought you were tailing someone. Who hired you?"

"I'm still not at liberty to say. I just wanted to know if you knew any more about Charles."

"Nothing more than what I told you."

"Thanks for returning my call."

After I hung up the phone, Roselyn asked, "What was that all about?"

"We were right. He's the person in the van that's following Charles. He said after Charles got home, he was confronted by a man in his driveway.

I wonder whether it could have been Jan's father. If it is, that means someone else is paying for the surveillance."

"That would eliminate Jan's father as the person that hired him," she replied. "I have a suspicion it's someone from the theatre, but who?"

"Your dinner's on the table. It won't be worth eating if I have to warm it twice," Ethel said.

After dinner we returned to the theatre for the second performance. Florence summoned everyone together, before the start of the show.

"I know what happened to Jan was a shock to everyone, but we still have a play to put on. There can't be another performance as there was this afternoon, or we might just as well end the play now. Everyone had better get back to business."

The cast reassured her there wouldn't be a repeat performance, and everything returned to normal.

In a few days Jan returned to everyone's delight, receiving accolades for her quick recovery. She seemed to have a better prospective, and Roselyn and I thought the extra attention Peter was paying to her may have been the reason.

The tension in the air between Cheryl and Peter didn't affect the performance, but back stage was a different atmosphere. There were harsh words between them at times when they thought no one was within hearing distance. From bits and pieces we could hear that Peter left Cheryl's apartment and found an apartment of his own.

On one particular incident when Roselyn and I were leaving the theatre, we heard Cheryl tell him, "You'll regret what you've done. Wait and see!"

Peter responded, "I never made a permanent commitment to you. It was just a temporary stopover. Whatever you conjured up in your mind is something you have to deal with."

Waiting in the parking lot for the car to warm up, we saw Cheryl exiting the theatre with Carl.

"Look, Allen, it doesn't seem like Cheryl's wasting any time with a replacement."

"Yes, she seems like an opportunist. She attracted Peter, helping him secure his part in the play for his attention, now Carl."

"Well, we can't dwell on it. It seems like Peter and Jan are happy with each other."

"I know. For all the time Peter and I were together, he never seemed this happy. He's like a different person."

Chapter 8

Within two weeks, Cheryl and Peter seemed to be over their differences, but it was replaced with Florence having a problem. Whatever it was, the falling attendance didn't help. Several times after the performance we heard her and Charles in the office having a few heated words about closing the play. It had only been running for a little over two months, but it was Florence's opinion the attendance was low due to inclement weather. Another point she used for keeping it open is that after Christmas, a lot of people don't visit the area again until early spring.

She must have been persuasive; he didn't close the show.

By the end of March, the attendance began to pick up again, and that crisis seemed to be over.

***

On a few occasions the past two months, we saw Cheryl and Carl together. It seemed as though the bad feelings between Cheryl and Peter had passed. Jan and Peter were now living together, and everything seemed to be back to normal.

Easter weekend was here, and the pleasant sign of budding trees and warmer weather was a welcoming site.

Roselyn and I made a few trips to the city when we had the opportunity, and Roselyn was adamant we didn't go as extravagant as our first trip, but it didn't make any difference. Every trip was as good as our first.

We had just gotten to our room in the city when Roselyn had the television on to listen to the weather report. I was in the shower when I heard her scream.

Fearing she fell, or something else that caused her to react, I leapt from the shower, almost falling. When I came out of the bathroom, she was face down on the bed crying.

I stood frantically looking around to see if anything was visible that would cause such a reaction.

"What's wrong? What happened?"

She sat up, literally shaking with her hands over her eyes. I repeated, "Roselyn, what is it?"

Removing her hands from her face, she looked up at me. "I just heard on the news Jan's dead. They found her body in the theatre."

"Jan? Jan Dougherty?"

"Yes, you better call and speak to someone. Find out what happened."

I called the theatre and Florence answered the phone.

"Florence, this is Allen. Roselyn and I are in the city. We just heard on the news that Jan was dead. What happened?"

"No one seems to know. Edward found her body behind one of the clothing racks in the prop room. Maybe you better come back. I'm sure there's going to be some questioning."

We gathered our things and hurried back to New Hope.

***

Arriving at the theatre, we saw a number of the cast cars in the parking lot. Going in, we saw everyone gathered in the audience seating area murmuring to one another.

"Florence, what happened?" Roselyn asked. "Edward, Florence said you found her body in the prop room."

"Yes, I was in such a rush to get home last night because my wife is sick," Edward replied. "I forgot to turn in my clothes and came back this morning. When I opened the door to give them to Jan, I didn't see her. I went up to the office, thinking someone might be here, but there wasn't. I thought she may have left, so I went in to hang them up myself. That's when I found her lying face down behind the third rack. She had a scarf tied around her neck. I didn't touch anything. I went back to the office and called the police."

"We're here because the police want to interview us. They should be here shortly," Florence said.

"Where's Peter?" Roselyn asked.

"We don't know. We can't contact him. Nobody seems to know where he is. I just phoned the police and told them for the exception of him, we're all here," Florence said.

Within 20 minutes Detective Kadelack arrived, accompanied by a state police detective. Knowing him from the encounter at the boarding house, I said hello.

Addressing the group he said, "I'm Detective John Kadelack. I'll be in charge of the investigation."

He pointed to the gentleman he came in with. "This is Detective Ben Davis from the state police. He'll be working with me. We'd like to interview you one at a time in the office, so if you bear with me, we can get this done relatively quickly."

Officer Davis was a stocky, barrel-chested individual in his mid 30s with thick, black curly hair.

"Detective, could you interview me first? My wife's at home sick," Edward asked.

He looked over our group. "I don't have a problem with that. I'm sure no one else would either."

After Edward's interview, they called Roselyn, then me. We gave our account of what we knew and hung around to talk to everyone else, wondering why Peter was so conspicuously absent. After Carl came out, he and Cheryl quickly left.

After I came out of the interview, Roselyn asked, "Did you mention Carl being at the Lambertville Tavern on New Year's Eve, or the private detective following Charles?"

"Yes, they seemed to be pretty interested in that," I said.

"Did you tell them anything about us overhearing the heated words between Cheryl and Peter, when she told him he would regret what he did?"

"Yes, I thought Peter might bring that out too when they interview him."

Detective Kadelack opened the office door and asked, "Has Peter Austin arrived yet?"

Looking around, Roselyn replied, "No, he hasn't."

"Well, we're finished for now, but we'll probably need more interviews."

Just as he was about to leave, Peter came rushing into the theatre to where we were seated.

"I'm Peter Austin. I understand you want to interview me?"

"Yes, if you'll go into the office, I'll be right there," Detective Davis said.

Hurriedly heading for the office, Detective Kadelack followed. Within 15 minutes, Peter came out again with a totally devastated look.

"Peter, where've you been?" Roselyn asked.

"I was in the city sitting at a bar when I saw the news. I rushed back as fast as I could. When the woman at my apartment told me the police were there, I called the police station. They said the detective was conducting interviews here. When I pulled up, Frank was just leaving. He told me they wanted to interview me. Does anyone know what happened?"

He seemed genuinely concerned. I replied, "I don't think they know anymore than she was dead, possibly by strangulation."

"How long was she dead before they found her?" Peter asked.

"I don't know, but from what Edward said, it couldn't have been that long. When's the last time you saw her?" I asked.

"I saw her here earlier, about 9. She was supposed to meet me at the apartment later this afternoon. We were going out to dinner to celebrate."

"Celebrate what?" Roselyn asked.

Taking a small box from his pocket, he opened it. "This. I intended to give it to her at dinner tonight. That's why I went to the city, to pick it up."

"It's a gorgeous engagement ring. Did Jan expect it?" Roselyn asked.

"I think she knew it was coming, but I don't think she expected it tonight."

"Peter, you're a paradox. I never thought you two were that intimate. I'm so sorry for you."

He replied holding the ring box as if he was somehow to blame for not being here, "If you'll excuse me. I'm heading back to the apartment. I think I want to be alone for awhile."

"Allen, I wonder if Jan's father's been informed?" Roselyn asked.

"I don't know. Does anyone know his address or phone number? Florence, you must have it on file. If you don't, I'm sure you have Charles phone number. Jan's father and him were partners in business. Has Charles even been informed?"

"I never thought to call him, but I'll do that now. I'll call Jan's father too. In fact, I'll give the police a copy of my rolodex file with everyone's phone numbers."

"Florence, will the play go on as scheduled Wednesday?" Roselyn asked.

"Yes, if Peter's not able to handle it, there's an understudy that might be able to. How do the rest of you feel?"

"We'll be fine, but we can't answer for Cheryl and Carl. They left after the interview," I said, after we all agreed.

"I'll catch up with them later. We still have until Wednesday afternoon before curtain call," Florence said.

"Well, Roselyn, there's nothing more we can do here. Let's go back to the boarding house."

Just as we were leaving, Detective Kadelack opened the office door and called down, "Allen, I'd like to ask you a few more questions."

After going back to the office I closed the door. Looking up at me he asked, "This private detective that was following Charles, did you speak to him?"

"Yes, he called the boarding house where I live and asked a few questions," I replied.

"When was that?"

"Just before Christmas, he wanted to know whether Roselyn or I ever saw Jan at the boarding house."

"Did he say why he wanted to know?"

"I asked who wanted to know and who hired him, but he said he wasn't at liberty to say."

"Do you remember his name?"

"If I can remember correctly, I think his name was Mike Taylor."

Kadelack looked at Davis. "I guess we'll have to find out who hired him."

"I hope he'll tell us; it's client protection. He doesn't have to say."

I had already told them about the van Roselyn and I saw in the parking lot at the theatre on New Year's Eve, and seeing it again when we were leaving the Lambertville Tavern. I told them we saw the van pull away a few moments after Charles left, and we thought he might be following him instead of Jan.

"You mentioned, you thought the van was following Charles and not

Jan. Why would you think he was following Jan?" Detective Davis asked.

"He called the boarding house one night and asked if I ever saw Jan there, that's why. I told him no, but the truth is about two weeks after the play began, Roselyn saw Peter sneaking Jan into his room one night."

Davis looked up at me. "Do you know whether they had a serious relationship at that time?"

"I don't know. At that time Roselyn and I thought Peter and Cheryl were having an affair."

"Why do you think that?"

"I was outside the prop room one evening getting ready to turn over my clothes when I heard Peter's voice in there talking to Jan. Whatever it was about made her upset. When I went in, I could see she'd been crying. I didn't see Peter, but I did see someone's feet standing behind a clothing rack. I assumed it was him. Roselyn knows Peter. She thought he got the part for the play by having personal influence with Cheryl. She let it slip that they were out to dinner the night before he got the part. We thought that might have been the reason. I talked to Peter several days later, and mentioned how upset Jan seemed to be. He reacted like it was his personal business and my input wasn't welcomed. Several days later, he moved in with Cheryl."

"When you told me she said she would get even with him, was it about him leaving her and getting an apartment with Jan?" Davis asked.

"I think so. I didn't see any other reason. They only got the apartment within the last month. There didn't seem to be any more hostile feelings between Peter and Cheryl, so everyone thought it passed. Has anyone notified Jan's father?" I asked.

"Yes, he's been away on business. He's expected back this afternoon. His wife said she would contact him. You can go. If there's anything else you remember, let us know. Thanks for the input."

Just as I was leaving, Charles arrived. "Is everyone still inside?" Charles asked.

"No, only Florence and the police are still there."

"Good. I want to speak to Florence. Where's Cheryl and Carl?"

"They left right after their interview."

Florence was just leaving her office when she saw Charles.

"Florence, I just heard about Jan. What happened?" Charles asked.

"Edward found her body in the prop room. I'm sorry. I can't talk right now. This whole thing's upsetting. You'll have to speak with the police. They're up stairs in the office."

"Do you think we'll have to close the play?" Charles asked.

"I spoke to everyone. I think we're fine. If Peter's still having a problem, I can call his understudy. Call me later. I'll be home."

After Charles knocked at the office door, Detective Kadelack opened it.

Charles took a seat in the office. "I'm Charles Cohen. You want to speak to me?"

"Just a couple questions; how are you connected to the theatre?" Davis asked.

"I own most of the shares in the theatre, and I'm the play's financier."

"When's the last time you saw Jan?"

"I saw her last evening," Charles replied.

"Here in the theatre?"

"No, we had a late snack together after the performance. We went to a tavern close by."

"What's your interest in Jan outside the theater?" Kadelack asked.

Alertly looking around, he seemed alarmed that the detective knew more about his personal life than he would have divulged.

"I've known her most of her life," Charles said, "Jan's father, Sam Dougherty, and I were partners in business. I got her the job here. I've been like a mentor to her for several years."

"You say you were partners with her father. What happened to the partnership?"

"We had a falling out over something that happened. I was married to Sam's cousin, and she committed suicide after we divorced. Sam blamed me for it."

"How did she commit suicide?"

"She shot herself."

"How long ago was that?"

"Five years ago. I've only seen him twice since then."

"When was the last time you saw him?"

"About two years ago."

"You said the last time you saw Jan was last night, but Cheryl said she saw you with her having coffee this morning. Is that true?"

"No. Well, yes. I forgot to mention it, but when I saw her going into the coffee shop, I went in. I didn't have coffee with her. I only asked if she would give the check for the cast's wages to Florence. She told me she had something important to do and couldn't, then I left."

"That's all we have to ask for now. We'll be in touch with you later if we have more questions."

As he was leaving the room, he looked over his shoulder. "If you do, you have my phone number. Just call me."

Kadelack said, "Ben, this Detective Taylor, we should tell him to come to police headquarters and give a statement."

"I was thinking the same thing."

Heading toward the theatre exit, Florence asked, "Are you leaving?"

"Yes, we're heading back to headquarters. If you can think of anything you might have missed let us know."

"The show opens again Wednesday, we'll be here," Florence replied.

A short time after they returned to the police station, there was a knock at the door. After opening it, Detective Kadelack was looking at a very distraught man, who said with a shaky voice, "Detective Kadelack, I'm Sam Dougherty. Where's my daughter?"

"Come in, Mr. Dougherty. She's at the medical examiner's office." Kadelack replied.

"What happened to her?"

"She was found dead in the prop room at the theatre. It appears she'd been strangled."

With downcast eyes he asked, "Was she molested in any way?"

"We don't think so. The medical examiner's report will tell us that."

Sam looked up asking, "Is Charles Cohen involved in any way?"

Looking surprised at his near accusation, Kadelack asked, "Why do you ask?"

"He's involved with the theater. I wouldn't put it past a guy like him."

"Why do you say that? I understand you were in some sort of business together."

"Yes, we had an importing business."

Detective Davis asked, "What was the breakup of the partnership about?"

"I didn't know you knew about that. Charles was married to my cousin. According to him, she committed suicide after their divorce, but I never believed him. I don't believe she would have done that. I was always suspicious of him being the one that did it. I always felt a little guilty because I was the one that got them together."

"When was the last time you saw him?"

"On New Year's Eve, I confronted him in his driveway about seeing my daughter."

"You mean seeing her on a personal relationship basis?"

"Yes, Charles always liked younger girls. They're the most vulnerable. I told that to Jan when I visited her at the hospital, but I don't think she took me seriously."

"How many relationships with younger girls have you known about?"

"At least four."

"Could you tell me who they were?"

"Yes, one was the secretary in the office of our business; another was a waitress from the club we belonged to; Cheryl that's in the theatre troupe here and..."

Detective Kadelack cut him off abruptly. "You mean he had a relationship with Cheryl too?"

"Yes."

Changing the subject Sam asked, "What will happen with Jan's body?"

"After the medical examiner's finished, we'll send her to whatever funeral parlor you want. Just leave the name with the secretary out front. One other question, two of the people from the theatre believe Charles was being followed by a private detective. Were you aware of that?"

"No, but it wouldn't surprise me. If there's nothing else I can help you with, let me know. I'd like to go now and make arrangements for my daughter."

"If we have any questions, we'll call. Again, we're very sorry we have to meet this way. Hopefully we can get to the bottom of it."

After he left the room, Kadelack said, "Ben, did you hear what he said about the last time he saw Charles? He said it was New Year's Eve. Charles told us it's been two years. Why would Charles lie about that?"

"I don't know, but I'm anxious to find out what that private detective has to say. Have you called his office?"

"Yes, he should be here this afternoon."

At 4 p.m. as Ben was about to leave, he was met at the door by a man identifying himself as Mike Taylor.

"I'm looking for Detective Kadelack. He wanted to speak to me. I'm a private investigator."

"Come in. I'm Detective Ben Davis from the state police." Pointing at Kadelack, he said, "He's Detective Kadelack, New Hope Police Department."

"Detective, what's this all about?" Mike asked.

"Jan Dougherty was found dead this morning in the theatre. We understand you've been following Charles Cohen. Who hired you?" Davis asked.

"I'm not at liberty to say until I ask the person. If they say it's okay, then I'll divulge the name."

"Allen Simpson told me he had a conversation with you about the beating Jan took on New Year's Eve. He said when you followed Charles home, he was confronted by a man in his driveway. He said you told him the confrontation was almost physical. Who was that person?"

"I don't know. I never interfered. I was only told to follow Mr. Cohen."

"Is there a specific reason?"

"I don't know that either. I was just being paid for doing it."

"Another question; as I mentioned, Jan was beat up pretty bad on New Year's Eve while you were on your surveillance of Charles. Did you happen to see anyone hanging around the Lambertville Tavern?"

"I remember seeing a man come out, light a cigarette, then walk around the corner. I remember seeing him look back around the corner at the entrance a few times as though he was waiting for someone. But as I said, my interest was following Charles."

"The person that came from the bar, can you give me a description?"

"He looked to be about 6 foot tall with dark hair. He was wearing a long, dark overcoat with the collar pulled up, that's about all. The only light to see by was the light from the front porch of the tavern, and from the street lights. After he went around the corner, I assumed he was just a patron that left. What attracted my attention that he was still there, he lit another cigarette, and I could see the glow when he inhaled. That's about it."

"Thanks for coming in. If the person that hired you would come forward, I'd appreciate it."

"I'll ask," Mike said and then he left.

"Ben, there's someone that's not telling everything they know. Number one: Charles told us a lie about not seeing Jan's father for two years. Number two: If Mr. Dougherty said he wouldn't be surprised if someone was following Charles, I don't think he'd be the person that hired Taylor. I wonder if there's something we may have missed back in the prop room. I think I'll call Florence and ask her to let me look again. Care to go with me?"

"No, I think I'll go to the boarding house and speak to Roselyn again. Maybe she can shed some light on Peter's past history. If you find anything in the theatre, call me."

Arriving at the theatre, Kadelack was met in the parking lot by Florence. She asked, "Officer Kadelack, do you want to go back in?"

"Yes, if you don't mind. I'd like to take another look around."

Unlocking the door, Florence asked, "Where do you want to look?"

"The prop room in particular. I want to look around the floor where Jan's body was found. I want to see if I missed anything."

"Do you want me to accompany you, or should I wait in my office?"

"You can wait in your office. I shouldn't be that long."

After opening the door to the room, he noticed the floor had been wiped clean.

As Florence was climbing the stairs to the office he asked, "Florence. It looks like the floor's been wiped. The chalk marks from the body position are wiped clean."

"I guess the janitorial service has been here. I called them after my interview. It was kind of eerie seeing it."

"Who does your cleaning service?"

"Delux. They're right here in New Hope."

"Do they always send the same people?"

"I don't know. Most of the time they come after we leave, unless we have a special request."

After returning to the prop room, he began looking at the clothing hanging on the racks. Seeing a long, dark overcoat as detective Taylor described on the man waiting outside the tavern, he searched the pockets and found a book of matches with the tavern logo. In another pocket he discovered a handkerchief with light red lipstick smudges. Taking out a small plastic evidence bag, he placed them inside.

Just then, Florence came to the door. "Are you almost finished?"

"Yes, Can I ask you a question? Does anyone in the cast ever take any of these clothes home?"

"They're not supposed to. Why do you ask?"

Keeping the discovery secret, he said, "No reason, just asking. I won't be too much longer."

"Okay, I'll be by the exit door."

As he closely examined the clothing rack, he found a white shirt with the sleeve torn at the cuff. It too had a smear of lipstick that seemed to be the same color as the handkerchief. Looking through the trousers on the rack, he noticed a pair of black trousers with what appeared to be some stains at the belt line. Finding a plastic bag, he gathered the articles, placing them inside, then headed for the exit.

"What do you have there?" Florence asked.

"I found some clothing I'd like to have checked. Do you mind if I take them with me?"

"Well, that looks like the outfit Carl uses for the play. How long will you need them? We open again day after tomorrow."

"I can't guarantee you'll have them back by then. Will that be a problem?"

"Yes, very much. We don't have a replacement, and that's the only one available. If you want to take the white shirt, fine. We can replace it. If you can wait till Sunday afternoon, that's the last performance of the week."

"That's out of the question. Whatever evidence that may be there might get contaminated and won't be useful. I hate to put pressure on the theatre, but I can get a warrant to have it taken."

"Then that's what you'll have to do. Are you finished?"

Taking the trousers and overcoat from the bag, he handed it to her.

"Thanks for the cooperation, I'll be back tomorrow with the warrant," he said sarcastically before leaving.

After returning to the police station, he called Ben. "Ben, I called Florence after you left and met her at the theatre. I looked over the wardrobe room. The floor had already been wiped clean. No chalk marks of the outline of the body-nothing! I searched the clothing rack and found a coat like the one Taylor described the guy was wearing coming from the tavern on New Year's Eve. I searched the pockets and found a book of matches with the tavern's logo. There was also a handkerchief with lipstick stains on it in another pocket. There was a white shirt there that had a slight tear on the sleeve and it also had a smudge of the same shade of lipstick. I asked Florence who wears the clothing in the play, she said Carl Dunn. When I asked if I could take them with me, she turned me down for taking the coat and suit, but let me take the shirt. I would have liked to have been able to take the suit trousers; they had stains around the belt line. It wouldn't surprise me at all if she gets them cleaned before we can have them. Sounds weird, don't it?"

"I wonder why she let you have the shirt and not the suit or overcoat," Ben said.

"Her excuse was she could replace that without a problem, but she couldn't replace the suit jacket and overcoat before the play resumes day after tomorrow. She told me I could have them at the end of the week, but I told her whatever evidence that might still be there would be contaminated when it's being used. To shake her up a little, I mentioned getting a warrant."

"What did she say to that?"

"She told me to get it."

"Did she say who cleaned up the chalk marks from the floor?"

"She said they have a cleaning service contract with a company called Delux. They're right here in New Hope. It's a pretty well-known business. I would guess they handle about half the office cleaning jobs here. As soon as I'm through talking to you, I'll give them a call."

"Best not waste any time. They'll probably be leaving to do their work. Most offices get cleaned during the evening hours. Get back to me after you speak with someone."

Kadelack dialed Delux's number. "Hello, is this Delux Cleaning Service?"

"Yes, it is. How can I help you?"

"I'm Detective Kadelack from the New Hope Police Department."

Before getting a chance to speak further, the voice replied, "Officer, if it's about anything missing?"

Kadelack abruptly interrupted. "No, it's not a complaint. Are you the owner of the company?"

"Yes."

"I was wondering who handles the cleaning at the New Hope Theatre."

"If it's about the girl that was killed, we'll be right out to clean up."

"You mean you haven't been there yet?"

"No, I just saw it on the news and was going out with the crew to personally supervise. Is it a bloody mess?"

"No, she was strangled. Do the same people usually handle the theatre?"

"Yes, we try to keep the same people doing the same places. It's less confusing."

"Can I have your name?"

"Henry, Henry Hardy."

"Henry, could I possibly meet you there?"

"I don't see why not. We're about to leave now. We'll be there in 15 minutes."

"Thanks, I'll see you then."

Kadelack redialed Ben's number.

"Ben, I just spoke to the owner of Delux. He said they haven't been there yet. I told him I'd meet him there. I want to catch them before they start cleaning. I told them not to bother with the prop room until I examined it further."

"Will you need me?" Ben asked.

"I don't think so, but it would be helpful if you could call Florence and try keeping her busy on the phone while I'm there with the cleaning people. The way she left, I can't trust what her motives might be. Telling me the janitorial service was already there when they hadn't, and her reluctance to let me have the suit and overcoat doesn't add up."

"Okay."

When Kadelack arrived at the theatre, the cleaning crew was already busy. It seemed as though they had it down to a science, everyone assigned to certain jobs.

Kadelack asked, "Are you Henry?"

"Yes, we haven't touched the prop room. Is there any other place we shouldn't bother right now?"

Henry was a short, portly, balding man in his early 50s. He had a stump of an unlit cigar dangling from his lips.

"Did anyone clean the office yet?" Kadelack asked.

"Wait a minute," calling out to one of the cleaning crew. "Alice, did you do the office yet?"

A middle aged woman wiping down the seating area replied in a raspy voice, "No Henry. I only have two hands. It doesn't help that your brother Mike didn't show up for work either."

Embarrassed, he said, "She's talking about my brother. He has a little bit of a drinking problem."

Kadelack smiled replying, "If you can just hold off on them for a few minutes, I want to take a look around."

Kadelack looked over the clothing in the prop room. The garments he wanted were missing. Florence hadn't returned them to the clothing rack. Why? Further examination revealed a light jacket lying on the floor under one of the racks. It didn't look like a piece of wardrobe that just slipped off a hanger. It looked like it was tossed haphazardly under the rack. Closer examination revealed a set of initials on the inside label: J. D.

He thought, "This must be Jan Doherty's jacket. It's probably the one she was wearing that day." Searching the pockets, he found a scrap of paper with a phone number. Taking a plastic bag, he placed the jacket in it then headed for the office, hoping to find the clothing he was refused.

Searching the office, the clothing he wanted was nowhere to be found. Did Florence take them with her? If she so desperately needed them for the performance, why weren't they still here? Suddenly, something caught his eye: an earring on the floor next to a filing cabinet. Examining it, he discovered it was bent. Remembering taking pictures in the prop room of Jan's body, he remembered she only had one earring.

Was she murdered here and dumped in the prop room?

Looking in the trash can he discovered a card from Mike Taylor's Detective Agency. He thought, "I wonder if she's the one who's having Charles followed?"

Tissues in the trash can, had lip stick smudges almost identical to the ones he saw on the shirt sleeve he was allowed to take earlier.

Picking up the phone, Kadelack dialed Ben. "Ben this is John. I'm at the theatre and the garments she wouldn't let me take aren't here. I did find a jacket tossed in a corner that probably belongs to the deceased. It has her initials on the inside label. It looks expensive. I also found an earring on the floor in the office. It looks like the missing earring to the one Jan had on. I was wondering if she may have been killed here and taken to the prop room."

Before continuing, Ben said, "John, I called Florence's number, but there was no answer. I don't know where she is, but I'd lay odds she'll return to the theatre at some point. Why don't you come back?"

Hanging up the phone, Kadelack could hear Florence outside the office door talking to the cleaning service boss. "Is he still here?" Florence asked.

"I think so, Miss Stark. I saw him go in the office."

Opening the door she said, "Detective, is there something else I can help you with? I have to make a phone call."

Kadelack looked around, "I was wondering where the suit and overcoat is. I didn't see them in the prop room?"

Looking embarrassed, she fumbled for words. "After I examined them, I thought it best if I got them cleaned before the performance. I didn't realize they were so dirty," Florence replied.

"Well, if you intended to let me have them at the end of the week, there's nothing to examine now. Any evidence would be gone," Kadelack said.

"You said you couldn't wait for the end of the week, and I didn't know how long it would take you for your examination. I just took it for granted you gave up on the idea of taking them. Sorry! I took them to the cleaners in town. They promised they could have them by tomorrow afternoon-What's in the plastic bag?"

"I think it's a jacket that belonged to Jan. I found it tossed in the corner in the prop room. It has her initials on the inside label," Kadelack said.

"I think it was Jan's. I saw her wearing it several times. Are you taking it?" Florence asked.

"Yes, I think I'll have it looked at just in case there's something that will be helpful with this investigation."

"Officer, could it have been someone that just got into the theatre and killed her?"

"I don't know. That's a possibility. Does anyone else have a key to the theatre?"

"Only Charles Cohen, Jan, and myself. The cleaning staff and lighting crew have keys too. What makes you ask that question? Do you suspect it's someone connected to the theatre?"

"To say that would be presumptuous. There's not that much to go on. If you can think of anything else in Jan's life that may be important, let me know. Thanks again for your cooperation," Kadelack said and then returned to the station.

Chapter 9

Several days passed since the incident at the office with Florence and Ben asked, "John, did you get the forensic report back yet?"

"Yes, Ben, it's just what we assumed. She died of strangulation, but chemical analysis of the stomach revealed a chemical."

"Does it say what kind?"

"It only gives the chemical analysis. I think it's pronounced chloral hydrate," Kadelack said.

"Does it say what the reaction to it is?"

"There's a notation here that refers to the next page," Kadelack turned the page. "It says blurred vision, drowsiness, passing out or trouble breathing. Sounds like whoever did it, was someone she knew. It's not like a recreational drug overdose. It was done on purpose. It's used on patients to put them in a semi-conscious state before surgery. Judging by the time of day, it would have been in a late breakfast drink or an early lunch beverage. There's something else too. Something on these pictures I don't quite understand," he said, taking out the photos.

"What's that?" Ben asked.

"There's a mark along the scarf line that stands out from the rest. Look!" Kadelack said.

"Let me see that scarf again," Ben said.

After examining the scarf Kadelack said, "There's nothing here that could have caused it. I wonder if something else was used and replaced by the scarf. I'd like to talk to Edward again. He's the one who discovered the body. Remember, the interview with him was short. His wife was sick."

"Why don't you call him and see if we could have an interview before the performance tomorrow? If he can point out anything, we'll be right there," Ben said.

Kadelack dialed Edward's number. "Hello, Edward? This is Detective Kadelack. Sorry to disturb you, but I didn't have time for a proper interview the other day. I'd like to get a more detailed account. By the way, how is your wife?"

"She's fine, thanks for asking. When would you like to meet?"

"If it's okay with you, could we meet sometime before the performance tomorrow?"

"I usually get there by noon, but I could make it earlier if you'd like, say around 10 o'clock. Would that be alright?"

"That will be fine, I'll see you then."

Kadelack hung up the phone. "Ben, he'll meet us there at 10. He told me Cheryl would open the theatre for us."

"Cheryl?"

"Yes, why?"

"I was just thinking. Florence told us only her, Charles Cohen, Jan, the cleaning company and the lighting and stage crew have keys. She never mentioned Cheryl having one."

"That's right!" he said, pausing for a moment, "She seemed pretty upset when we spoke to her though. Maybe she just forgot."

***

At 10 the following morning Edward pulled into the parking lot.

"Good morning, Edward. Is Cheryl coming to open the theatre?"

"I called her last night after talking to you. She told me to stop by her apartment and get the key this morning." Edward held it up. "Here it is."

Entering the darkened theatre, detective Kadelack asked, "Edward, let's start at the beginning. If you remember, try going over the same steps the day you found Jan."

He began recounting his steps that day. "When I pulled into the parking lot and didn't see her car, I just thought she wasn't here yet. She's usually the last one to leave and the first to arrive. I tried the door just for the heck of it and was surprised when it opened. I thought at first she just forgot to lock it the night before when she left. After I came in, I called out. 'Is anybody here?' But I didn't get an answer."

Ben asked, "Do you remember if there were any cars on the lot?"

"There's always a few, but that's normal. Sometimes people park here when there's no performance, just to walk down to look at the river. There's a small platform that gives you a nice view. A lot of people take pictures with the river as a background."

"Did you notice if any of the cars belonged to the cast?" Ben asked.

"I wasn't really looking. I was only interested in Jan's car."

"So you're telling us it wasn't here?" Ben asked.

"It wasn't in her reserved spot, no," Edward replied.

"Sorry for the interruption. Go on."

Reaching the back of the theatre, Edward continued, "As I said, I came in through the same door we just came through and went directly to the prop room. I knocked, but I didn't get an answer, so I pushed open the top half of the door. I didn't see Jan, so I closed it again. I thought, maybe she's in the office. So I went up to see. The door was locked, so I went back down to the prop room. As I was coming down the stairs, I heard someone push open one of the side doors along the last row of seats. You know; the push bar doors for a quick exit in case of a fire. They're kind of noisy."

"Did you see who it was?"

"No, I called out thinking it may have been Jan. If it was, she sure would have heard me. As I said, she's generally the last one to leave and the first to arrive."

"Did the door remain open?"

"No, it's one of those self-closing doors. It closes kind of slow. Funny, though..."

"What's that?" Ben asked.

Edward looked down at the floor. Searching his memory, he looked up. "I never thought of it till now. I came in through the door we came through. It wasn't locked. If it was Jan, she would have exited that door to lock it again after going out. It's the only side entrance that opens with a key. You have to physically lock it. It doesn't lock on its own, so it couldn't have been her."

John and Ben looked at each other suspiciously. Ben asked, "Then, what did you do?"

"I went to the prop room and knocked again." Edward thought. "No, wait. When I got to the prop room, the top half of the door was open again. I remember closing it just before I went up to the office. Someone must have been in there."

"Okay, you didn't see Jan so what did you do?" Ben asked.

"I called out to her again, and when I didn't get an answer, I opened the door all the way and went in. I hung my clothes on a hanger and was about to put them on the rack when I saw her feet. She was face down, and I thought at first she may have just fainted, so I bent down to wake her. When I loosened the scarf, her head tilted to one side. That's when I realized she was in trouble, she wasn't breathing. Her eyes were open and I felt for a pulse, but I couldn't feel one."

"Then what did you do?"

"I immediately phoned for an ambulance and the police."

"Do you remember if she was still warm?"

"Yes, like I said, I thought she just passed out. It must have happened minutes before I came in."

Ben asked, "When you knocked at the door the first time, did you notice anything out of place?"

"No, but after I came back and found her, there was one thing I did notice."

"What was that?"

"She was always particular with the props and made sure they were always hung up neatly. When I bent down to look at her, I could see several prop pieces on the floor under one of the racks. She would have never left them like that."

"Do you remember what they were?"

"Yes, one of the items was a sailor's cap and black scarf, the kind sailors wear on their dress white uniforms. The other things were a boatswain's whistle and a white knotted rope from a ship's bell."

Kadelack asked, "They're not used in the play currently are they?"

"No, they were part of a play that ran before Murder at the Logan, the one I'm in."

"How do you know?"

"I saw it with my wife last summer."

"Did you pick them up?"

"No, after the ambulance left and the police arrived, I went home to my wife."

"Anything else you can remember?"

"I do remember seeing some black scuff marks on the floor."

"What kind of marks?"

"The kind you see when someone drags their feet across a wooden floor."

The three of them headed for the exit. "Thanks, Edward. That's about all. Will you be locking up the theatre now?" Ben asked.

Edward looked at his watch. "It's 11 o'clock now. I don't know what time Florence gets here. The theatre is always open when I arrive."

At that moment, the door slowly opened. Looking in that direction, it was Florence.

"What on earth are you doing here? I was about to call the police. I thought someone broke in."

Kadelack replied, "No, we wanted to ask Edward a few questions. We're leaving now. If there's anything else Edward, we'll let you know."

Florence said, "Edward, while you're here, I want to talk to you about your part in the play."

"Certainly, should we use the office?"

After the detectives left, they walked toward the prop room. Edward asked, "What did you want to speak to me about?"

"I really didn't have anything to say about your part in the play. I was just wondering what they were asking you?"

"They questioned me about finding the body and what I saw that day."

"Anything in particular?" Florence asked.

"I told them as much as I could remember, and about whoever was in the theatre when I went to the office to find Jan."

"What do you mean? Was someone else here?"

"There must have been. When I was coming back down from the office, someone exited one of the side doors. It was still closing when I yelled out. I thought it might have been Jan, but she would have never exited that door. She would have used the door we always come in."

"Did they ask anything else?"

"Just about the position of the body and the few things I saw on the floor."

"What things?"

"The navy cap, and scarf. The boatswain's whistle, and the white rope from the ship's bell."

"Where were they?" Florence asked, looking surprised.

"They were on the floor near Jan's body."

"I wonder how they got there. They're usually kept in the closet."

Edward replied, "I never thought of that. I wonder if the person that exited the theatre was hiding in there the first time I knocked. I never went in. I went straight to the office to see if she was there."

"Why did you come back to the theatre in the first place?"

"I forgot to hand in my clothes. I hurried home because my wife was sick. What did you want to tell me about my part?"

"Oh! It's no big deal. Forget it."

The cast began to arrive at noon, and gathered at the prop room.

Florence announced, "You'll have to get your own outfits until I can find someone else to control things. Try to remember to hang them back in the same place." She looked around, "Has anyone seen Carl?"

Looking at each other, we hadn't noticed he was missing.

Florence repeated, "Has anyone seen Carl?"

Without an answer, she turned, heading for the office, mumbling to herself. "What the hell are we going to do for a replacement this late in the day? Maybe Charles was right: Maybe we should just shut the damn play down."

Just then, Carl entered. "Sorry I'm late."

Florence adamantly asked, "Where the hell have you been? I was just about to call your understudy."

"The detectives came to the apartment. They had a few more questions."

Florence asked, "Carl, can we talk after the performance?"

"Sure, why not. Just let me change clothes first."

Edward told him, "Everyone has to get their own clothes."

"I assumed that."

Going to the rack where his garments were usually hung, Carl looked at the male cast members. "Has someone taken my clothes from the dressing room?" Looking at the male cast members, "Peter, Allen, have you seen them?"

"Aren't they there?" Allen asked.

"No."

"Florence is in the office. Maybe she knows where they are," I said.

Carl knocked on the office door... "Come in."

Opening it wide enough to get his head in, Carl asked, "Florence, where are my clothes?"

"I sent them to the cleaners. They promised they would have them by the performance," she replied.

Carl stepped into the office. "Were they that soiled? I didn't think they were that bad that they needed cleaning."

"I thought so. They took the white shirt, though. I bought another after I spoke to them yesterday."

"Who took the white shirt? What the hell's going on?" Carl demanded.

"The police took it. They wanted to take the suit and overcoat too, but I wouldn't let them. I bought you another white shirt."

"Why did they want my clothes?"

"I guess they want to examine the one you use."

"Examine it? Why?" Carl asked.

"There was a tear on the sleeve and a lipstick smudge on it. I think they want to see if it matches the lipstick Jan was wearing."

Looking puzzled at her remark, he asked, "Do they think I had something to do with it?"

"I don't know. Maybe you should ask them."

"I think I'll phone them after the play."

Florence took him by the arm in an endearing gesture, leading him to the office door.

"Carl," she said, "If there's anything I can help you with, let me know, anything at all!"

Carl abruptly stopped, "Wait a minute. You don't think I had anything to do with it, do you?"

"Let's just say we're friends, and I don't want to see anything happen to you."

"I don't know why you think the way you do, but I assure you I had nothing to do with it."

Closing the door again before he exited, Florence asked, "Weren't you and Jan seeing each other around Christmas? You came together to the Lambertville Tavern on New Year's Eve."

"Yes, but that was only her doing me a favor. My car wouldn't start when I left the theatre that night, and Jan was locking the door when she saw me trying to start it. She volunteered to drive me. If you were taking notes, you would have noticed I didn't leave with her."

"Yes, I remember, but that was the night she was beat up," Florence said. She paused. "Mike Taylor," she stopped abruptly.

"Who's Mike Taylor?" he asked.

"Just a friend, forget about it."

After removing her hand from his arm, he left the office, returning to the prop room. "Has anyone seen my suit?"

Edward replied, "Carl, I think it's in the dressing room. The dry cleaner just delivered something."

Heading for the dressing room he replied, "Florence said she sent it out to be cleaned, that must be it."

"You better hurry. The plays about to begin," Peter said.

Chapter 10

During the intermission, I asked, "Carl, Is something bothering you?"

"Why do you ask, Allen?"

"You missed a few lines during the first half. I was just wondering if it had anything to do with being upset about Jan's death."

"Very upset," he replied. "Can we talk after the play? I thought we could go somewhere and have coffee between performances."

"Why don't we go to the coffee shop on Main Street?" I asked.

"Thanks, Allen," He replied.

During the last half of the play, Carl seemed to be back to normal reciting his lines. Obviously relieved about our meeting, I wondered what was so traumatic that a mere meeting would trigger that kind of response.

After the curtain went down, we remained in our costumes and were heading out the door when Roselyn asked, "Allen, are we going to get a bite?"

"Carl and I are going to the coffee shop. He wants to talk to me."

"What about?" Roselyn asked.

"I don't know? Something's upsetting him. I guess I'll find out."

"I knew he must be bothered about something. He missed a few lines in the first half. Well, I'll see you later. I just might get something light and eat here," Roselyn said.

Kissing her lightly on the lips, I said, "Don't worry. I'll let you know what it is."

Getting to the coffee shop, Carl and I ordered our beverage and found a table in the rear of the room.

"Ok, Carl, what's going on..."

He didn't give me the chance to finish my sentence. He shocked me with his next few words.

"Allen, Florence thinks I had something to do with Jan's death," he said.

"Why would she think that?" I asked.

"I don't know, but when we were in the office before the performance, she grabbed my arm and said, she wouldn't want to see me in any trouble. When I told her I didn't have anything to do with it, she mentioned about Jan and I having an affair."

"Well, were you?" I asked.

"We had a few brief meetings around New Year's but nothing serious. I knew she was still head over heels with Peter, and I think she was using me to make Peter jealous. Florence said she noticed we went to the New Year's party together, and when I said if she was keeping tabs, she would have noticed we didn't leave together."

"Do you think she was keeping tabs on you? Maybe it was on Jan?"

"I don't know, but it made me feel awful uncomfortable. When the police questioned you and Roselyn, did they ask whether you knew about a relationship between Jan and me?"

"No, I never knew you had one. Oh! we saw you together a few times and saw you come with her on New Year's Eve like Florence, but that's it. I don't know what Roselyn was asked. I don't know if she mentioned you making unwanted advances to her, almost to the point where she was afraid."

"Yes, that wouldn't make me look good if I get accused, but as soon as you told me you two were an item, I dropped the advancement. Do you think Florence knew about that?" Carl asked.

"I don't know if Roselyn ever mentioned it to her. She may have, since she's the director. Do you want me to ask?"

"Well, it would ease my mind considerably, and if she didn't, that means she was getting false information from another source."

"I'll let you know after the performance tonight. Aren't you going with Cheryl now?"

"Yes, we began seeing each other shortly after Valentine's Day. She was pretty down about breaking up with Peter. That's when we got together. We've been living together for the last two months. Florence knows that, so where she gets her ideas from, I don't know."

"Did Florence ever make a gesture to want to have a relationship with you?"

"Other than going to the coffee shop a few times and out to dinner once, I never thought it was anything other than interest in my acting skills. Her knowledge with her stage experience has been really helpful."

"Carl, I'll find out what I can. I'll let you know."

"Thanks, Allen, I appreciate it."

After leaving the coffee shop, we returned to the theatre.

As soon as Roselyn saw me, she anxiously asked, "What was the meeting about?"

"Carl wanted to know if you told Florence about him making unwanted advances to you," I replied.

"No, I never mentioned it to anyone but you. Why?" Roselyn asked.

"It's a little complicated to get into now. We'll talk about it after the performance. I want to clear a few things up for Carl."

Looking bewildered, she said, "Do you mean the three of us getting together?"

"Why? Don't you feel comfortable in his company?"

"Not really."

"Well, I'll be there, so it should be alright. I think it's necessary because of what he told me about Florence."

She looked me in the eye. "Now I hope I don't forget any of my lines," she said.

***

After the play ended, we met with Carl at the theatre exit. Cheryl, seeing us together, joined the group.

"Are we going for a bite to eat?" Cheryl asked.

"No, Cheryl. I have something I want to discuss with them. I won't be very long. I'll see you at the apartment," Carl replied.

Concerned at why she wasn't included asked, "Whatever it is, maybe I can help."

"I don't think so. I'll discuss it with you later," Carl replied.

Looking annoyed at the rejection, she shoved open the door.

Watching her reaction, brought me back to the incident I saw at the hospital, when Peter chose to stay a little longer with Jan.

"Carl, I think you'll have a lot of explaining to do when you get home," I said.

Heading for the car, we saw Charles pulling into the parking lot.

Exiting his car he asked, "What's with Cheryl? I just said hello and she told me to go F myself, then got into her car and sped off. What gives?" Charles asked.

"I think she's pissed that were going to the Tavern to discuss something, and she wasn't invited," I said.

Surprised at my answer, he asked, "Is Florence still inside?"

"Yes, I think she's in the office talking to one of the lighting crew."

"Good, I'd like to speak to them too," Charles said.

After getting in the car, Carl turned to Roselyn and said, "I know you must feel uncomfortable in my company, and I'm grateful you came along. If you two think going for coffee without Cheryl is undermining the relationship I have with her, forget it. Our relationship isn't going to last much longer."

"Why not?" Roselyn asked.

"Did you see her reaction? That's the way she is most of the time. She's a control freak. If she can't be the dominant one, it really bothers her. I'm afraid our relationship is coming to an end."

"Well, let's get to the Tavern. We can discuss it," Roselyn said.

Upon entering, we went to the lower level and found a table, away from the bar area.

"That looks like a perfect spot," I said.

After ordering a light snack and liquid refreshments, Roselyn began the conversation.

"Carl, what did you want to ask me?" Roselyn asked.

Hesitatingly he replied, "Did Allen tell you anything about our meeting?"

"Not really, he said it would be better if we discussed it together."

"Well, the long and the short of it. I think Florence thinks I had something to do with Jan's death."

Surprised, she asked, "What makes her think that?"

"I don't know, but being pushy about confronting you with going out, doesn't look good if I'm looked at. Did you mention it to her?"

"No, I only asked Cheryl if she ever had any problems with you."

"I'm beginning to see now, that's where it probably came from. She must have told Florence."

Focusing on our conversation, we never noticed Cheryl coming in our direction.

"Okay, Carl, what the hell is the big secret!" she said, loud enough to attract the attention of the other patrons.

Embarrassed, with her remark Carl replied in a normal tone, "Keep your voice down. You know, we're not married. I don't have to answer to you. You're not my mother. I told you I'd let you know what it was about when I get back to the apartment."

Continuing in a loud voice, she answered, "You're right. I'm not your mother, but I am the one that pays the god damn rent among other things. Maybe you should look elsewhere for a sucker."

Roselyn looked around at the other patrons focusing on Cheryl's outburst, commenting in a quiet tone, "Cheryl, it isn't something you should get angry about. Don't say something you may regret later."

"You mean like him getting abusive when we're having sex?" Cheryl said.

Again, she said it loud enough for the patrons to turn and look.

Embarrassed, Carl replied, "Well, this certainly isn't the place to discuss it. Shall I find another place to stay tonight, or am I still welcome?"

The statement seemed to temporarily quell her anger. "Where will you go?" Cheryl asked.

"I could always go back to the theatre. Florence has a small cot she uses when she stays there."

"Cot? Where is it? I never knew she had one there," Cheryl asked.

"It's in the closet in the prop room," Carl replied.

"That's a new one on me," she said.

Her anger seemed to have dissipated once again.

"If you want to come back to the apartment tonight, you can," she said in a quieter tone.

As she walked away, Carl in a low tone remarked, "See what I mean about being domineering? She's like that most of the time."

"She brought out an interesting point. How is it she didn't know about the cot in the prop room? It seems like she knows almost everything else about the theatre," I asked.

"She's lying." He looked at Roselyn, embarrassed. "We used it once."

"Used it? You mean you and Cheryl, or you and Florence?" I asked.

His face, red with embarrassment, was easily identifiable in the dimly lit room.

"Now that we figured out who told who, Allen, I think we should be heading back," Roselyn said.

"I think you're right. Carl, I hope this clears things up for you," I said.

"If you don't have anything else you can tell me, I guess so," he replied.

Heading back to Ethel's, I asked, "Roselyn, Do you think Carl's telling the truth?"

"I think he's telling us as much as he wants. I think he used the cot with Florence too and maybe Jan. His face looked awful embarrassed when he said it. It also makes him look bad when she said he gets abusive when they're having sex. I wonder if he has any past history of physical abuse on women? I heard Florence mention to Cheryl he was divorced."

"That's a good question. Maybe the police should look into it? If he has, maybe he's the one that beat Jan," I said.

"He said he told Florence if she was checking on him, he didn't leave with her."

"No, but that doesn't mean he didn't meet her later," Roselyn replied.

"That's a possibility. They may have met later at the theatre."

"Allen, I think the next time we see Detective Kadelack, we should drop a hint about investigating his past."

"It has to be an unofficial suggestion. I don't really want to get caught up in this thing," I replied.

Turning to look at me, she was obviously upset at my statement and said, "Don't want to get caught up in this thing? What are you saying? It's the murder of a young girl we both knew and cared about."

"Take it easy. I don't mean that we shouldn't be concerned. Let's just be careful of what we accuse someone of doing," I said.

She realized my concern wasn't a dismissal of Jan's death, only a precaution against possibly being accused of pointing the finger of guilt. I could see by her facial expression, she was satisfied with my response, and I felt relieved.

We got back to the boarding house, but for me, a different feeling prevailed. Roselyn brought up a good point, and instead of feeling sympathetic to Carl, I began to look at him with suspicion. 'Did he have something to do with it? Was it an unintended consequence of a sex act?'

It seemed to fit right into the play we were performing. Peter's role was being the unintended murderer of the maid. Peter. I almost forgot. He was the one hiding behind the clothing rack the first time, after I heard their conversation.

Did he show us the ring to make us believe he couldn't be a suspect? He said the reason he was late getting to the theatre, is that he was in the city sitting at a bar when he heard the news about Jan.

Wait a minute, if he heard it while he was in a bar, it would have to have been the noon newscast. Did it take him four hours to drive the 35 miles? I'm sure if it was something that happened to Roselyn, I would have been here within an hour, maybe an hour and a half max. I laid my theory aside after we got in the house.

After kissing Roselyn lightly on the cheek, I said, "Goodnight." and began to climb the stairs. Grabbing me by the sleeve, she turned me around.

"Is that the best goodnight kiss you can muster? Maybe I should look for another dance student," she jokingly added.

It snapped me out of my thoughts.

"I'm sorry. My mind was on something Carl said. I wouldn't want you to take Wally the gardener as a partner. Remember, he's a married man."

We both laughed, then I gave her a proper kiss before retiring.

The following afternoon when we arrived at the theatre, we were surprised to see Detective Kadelack coming from the office.

It was close to 11:30, so we knew it had to be something important. We stood around looking at each other, curious about what he wanted.

When Florence stepped from the office, she looked down at us and said, "Allen, Detective Kadelack has a few more questions he'd like to ask you."

After looking at one another, Edward asked, "All of us or just Allen?"

"I think he only wants to speak with Allen. The rest of you can go to the prop room. I'll be there in a few minutes," Florence said.

As I walked up the stairs, Detective Kadelack seemed to look at me as though I was harboring some sort of suspicion. I looked back at Roselyn over my shoulder and said, "I shouldn't be too long. Wait for me."

"Ok, Allen, and don't forget what we discussed," Roselyn said.

"I won't. It's the best opportunity to do it. The timing's perfect," I replied.

As I opened the door to the office, I looked down at the group and saw Carl approach Roselyn. I paused for a moment to listen. I heard him ask if what I said about perfect timing had anything to do with our meeting.

Looking up at me wondering how she should answer that question, I heard her say, "When Allen comes down, you can ask him."

Entering the office I closed the door and took a seat.

Detective Kadelack asked, "When you were in the city and heard the news, how long did it take you to get back to the theatre?"

He read Roselyn and my mind with that very same question.

"It took us about an hour and a half from the time we checked out of the hotel. Why?" I asked.

"When I interviewed Peter, he said he was in a bar in Philadelphia when he heard the news and said he came straight up. He would have had to hear it on the 12 o'clock news. It wouldn't have taken him that long to get here."

"Well maybe he had to pick up the ring first."

"Pick up what ring?"

"When he got here that afternoon, he showed us an engagement ring he was going to give Jan that evening. That's why he went to the city- to pick it up."

Kadelack replied, "I never asked why he was in the city to begin with, but I hardly think he would be concerned with picking up a ring for a dead girl."

He was right. "Is Peter a suspect?" I asked.

"Yes, at this point they're several suspects. Can you tell me anything about Carl Dunn?" Kadelack asked.

Suspicious that Cheryl may have called him after our meeting, prompting this late-night interview, I chose to mention it. "Yes, Roselyn and I met with him after the first show. He wanted to ask us a few questions."

"What were the questions?"

"He wanted to know if Roselyn mentioned to Florence about his unwanted advances."

"And did she?"

"Not according to her. She said she only mentioned it casually to Cheryl, is that who told you?"

Tapping a pencil on the desk, I could see he was hesitant to answer. Avoiding my question but looked up, asking, "Do you know anything about Carl's life before meeting him here? Something he may have mentioned?"

"I did hear he was divorced, but that didn't come from him. Cheryl confronted us at the meeting and in her angry triad at him, she mentioned him being abusive in their relationship, but I took that as her being angry that she wasn't invited to the meeting.

In fact, she got pretty loud with it," I said throwing a hint that Carl may be abusive without actually pointing a finger.

"What do you mean loud with it?" Kadelack asked.

"It attracted the attention of everyone around us," I replied.

"You said abusive. Did you ever see bruises or marks on Jan?"

"Yes, I noticed them once."

"Did you question her about them?"

"No, I didn't think it was appropriate. Our relationship never extended further than the theatre- and very little personal contact when we were here."

"Did you ever see her in the company of Charles Cohen away from the theatre?"

"Yes, a few times."

"Could you tell me about them?"

"I was coming back to the theatre after buying coffee one afternoon and saw her getting out of his car, and what sounded like the end of a heated conversation."

"What did you hear?"

"After she got out, she stood with the door open and I heard her say in a loud voice, 'Damn it, I told you before, you're not my father!' Then she slammed the car door. She was heading to the theatre door when I called to her, but she ignored me and went inside. I asked her later about it, and she just blew off my question, as if it was none of my business.

That's the day I saw someone standing behind the clothing rack after the last performance. They obviously didn't want to be seen."

"You mean- like hiding?"

"I don't think that. They had to know their lower legs were exposed. They had to realize I could see that, or maybe they just thought I wouldn't notice. It could be they just didn't want me to know who they were," I replied.

"Do you remember whether Peter and Jan were involved in a relationship at the time?"

"I can't remember. I think they've been in and out of a relationship since the play opened. Is there anything else you wanted to ask?"

"You said you heard Carl was divorced. Do you know where he was living at the time?"

"No, maybe someone else would have that information. Cheryl should know. She's probably the one that told you about him being abusive."

Still not answering my question about the informer he said, "Thanks for the interview. Sorry to have kept you so late."

"This is unusual. Is there pressure from somewhere to get this resolved?"

He gave me a look that let me know I struck a nerve.

Leaning back in his chair he looked at me and said, "Yes, as a matter of fact, we're getting pressure from higher up in the department, both in the county and the state."

"Do you know where the pressure's coming from?" I asked.

"I assume its Jan's father Sam. He wields a lot of power in the world of business, especially around here. Thanks again for the interview. Could you ask Roselyn to come in?"

I left the room and asked Roselyn to go to the office. As she passed, she wanted to know whether I could be with her during the interview.

"I don't think so. I think he wants separate interviews about meeting Carl, that's mainly what we discussed."

Her interview was brief, and within 5 minutes she came down the stairs with the detective.

On the way home, she affirmed my suspicion that he wanted to know more about being confronted by Carl.

"What did you tell him?" I asked.

"I told him I was afraid by the way Carl approached me, and how I had to physically move him out of the way so I could pass."

"Did he ask anything else?"

"Yes, he asked me if I knew where Carl lived before he came here."

I replied, "He asked me the same question. I told him he'd have to ask someone else. I didn't know."

I was surprised when she looked at me and said, "He's from a small town northwest of Philadelphia. Pennsburg, I think she said."

"Who said?" I asked.

"Florence. You know, it's not looking too good for Carl. I think Cheryl has a lot to do with this too."

"I think you're right."

Chapter 11

Several days passed without any police presence and things began to return to normal. By Friday, Roselyn and I were looking forward to our days off we missed the previous week.

At 3 p.m. on Friday, Detective Kadelack returned to the theatre with Detective Davis and announced, "Carl, I'd like to interview you at the end of the second performance."

"Only me?" Carl asked.

"For now yes. That is, unless you prefer to come to the police station in the morning," Detective Davis said.

"Whatever you want to ask, let's do it today." Carl was cut short.

In a raised voice, Florence said, "Detective, these people have to remember their lines. It's disrupting enough to have had Jan murdered here, but the cast must perform as the audience demands. Is there any way this can be put off until Monday?"

"I can't do that. What I have to discuss with Carl is urgent," Davis replied.

Carl quickly responded, first looking at Florence then back at the detective, "Then I'll meet you in the office after the second performance."

"That will be good. I'll see you then."

Everyone wondered why Carl was singled out. If there were questions that couldn't wait, it must have been something they just discovered, and the room began to buzz with quiet conversations as to why.

Carl, nervously embarrassed at being singled out, looked at the rest of the cast.

"Don't look at me as though I was guilty of something," he shouted opting not to finish his statement.

"Carl, no one's accusing you of doing anything. Don't be so upset with our quiet conversation," I said.

As Florence took him by the arm leading him away from our group, I commented to Roselyn, "Look, she's doing the same thing again that Carl told us about. I wonder if she's taking him aside to reassure him of her support."

"That's probably what it is. I wouldn't know why she thinks he needs it, unless she knows something more about his relationship with Jan," Roselyn said.

At 9:30 p.m. Detective Kadelack and Detective Davis returned. Going to the office, Detective Kadelack asked Florence if he could use the room again for the interview.

"Certainly, is Carl going to be able to continue with the play, or should I get his understudy?"

She seemed to be prying about the questions, using Carl not being able to continue.

"If you're asking me whether he's going to be arrested? No he isn't. We only want to clear up a few things. Have you ever heard Carl speak about his life before coming here?" Kadelack asked.

Pausing for a moment, realizing it was a sensitive question she said, "We went to dinner a few times and he told me he was divorced, but that's about all I know."

"Did he ever mention living in a town called Pennsburg? It's northwest of the city."

"He did mention that as I recall, why?"

"It's something we want to discuss with him. Would you tell him we're here when he's finished?"

Turning in his direction before leaving the room, Florence said, "Yes, I'll tell him."

Twenty minutes later, Carl came in the office.

"Carl, have a seat. We just want to ask you a few questions," Kadelack said.

"Is this something I should have a lawyer present for?" Carl asked.

Kadelack and Davis looked at each other. "Not unless you feel you're in jeopardy of being charged with anything," Kadelack replied.

"Then go ahead. I have nothing to hide."

"You resided in a town called Pennsburg, Pennsylvania, didn't you?"

"Yes, but you already know that, why?"

"Were you living at 1225 Lakeside Road when you were married?"

"As a matter of fact, yes, I was."

"How long were you married?"

"Joan and I were married for about 8 years."

"Can you tell us about your marriage? Things like did you have any children? Was the divorce amicable?" Kadelack asked.

"No, we didn't have children, but yes, our divorce was amicable. My wife and I just didn't get along after I became unemployed. *White Printing Company* was a large printing facility in our town that closed. They moved to another state. I didn't want to relocate, so I left. I was unemployed for about six months. That's when she kept hounding me to find work. I was being paid well at *White* and couldn't find employment that paid that much, so I took a job at a local auto agency as a salesman for awhile, but that didn't pan out either."

"And that was the only reason for the divorce?"

"Yes."

"As a routine, I called the police department in Pennsburg and asked if they had any reports of being called to your residence."

Kadelack looked down at a folder.

"They had on file, several incidents of domestic disturbances. One report mentioned being summoned by neighbors that heard some loud yelling and screaming. It further stated there were signs of bleeding from Mrs. Dunn's mouth by the officer that arrived at the scene, but she refused to file a complaint. Is that correct?"

"Yes, but that was accidental. I was only trying to defend myself."

"Did you move here right after the divorce?"

"No, I stayed in the area for awhile- then got a license and began selling real estate. I did that for about a year. That's when I moved to Allentown. I got remarried to a woman from there."

"Yes, I have that here too. Her name was Ruth. Did you divorce her also?"

Carl looked down at the floor then slowly raised his head to face the detective. "No she died."

"Can you tell me about that?" Kadelack asked.

"Yes, as I was backing the car in the garage one night after we came back from a party, she told me to stop. There was a small table she used for her art work behind the car. After she got out, my foot accidently slipped off the brake, and the car went backwards, pinning her against the garage wall. She died that same night."

"Is that when you relocated?"

"Not right away. I had to settle the estate and get things in order. I just didn't want to live in that house. It really bothered me."

"Did Ruth have any relatives?"

"Yes, she had a sister and brother. They were part of the reason I left."

"Why's that?"

"I think they sort of blamed me for the accident. You know, being drunk and all."

"Is that when you moved here?"

"It wasn't too long after that- maybe six months."

"Ok, that's all I wanted to ask. Oh wait, have you ever been in the prop room? Not the front where the garments are hung, but the large room where they keep accessories?"

"No, I only went in the..." He stopped short of admitting he was in the part where the costumes were.

"That's all I wanted to ask. You can go."

Leaving the room, Carl wondered why he was singled out, but opted not to ask.

After he left, John sat on the edge of the desk looking through the case folder.

"Ben, I think he knows more about that storage room than he admits. I'm looking at something else here we discussed before."

"What's that?"

"Remember when you ran your hands over the scarf? It was smooth."

"Yes, I remember. We thought the marks on the neck couldn't have come from that. What are you thinking?"

"Remember Edward telling us that the ship's white bell rope had knots on it and was lying on the floor with the black scarf and the ship's bell. I wonder whether that white bell rope could have been used?"

"Well, let's ask Florence if we can take it for analysis," Ben said.

"It shouldn't be a problem. It isn't something they're using for this play. Maybe we can get a few more answers along with the analysis of the shirt."

Looking at his watch, Detective Davis said, "It's getting late. Let's get it and get out of here."

Going downstairs they confronted Florence.

"Florence, there were a few things on the floor in the prop room when Edward found Jan's body. One of the items was a braided white rope from the ship's bell. We'd like to take that with us for analysis, if you don't mind." Kadelack said.

"No problem," she replied.

Getting to the prop room, she opened the door to the storage closet. Moving items around, searching for the rope, she said, "It doesn't seem to be here. Are you sure it was put back?"

"That's something we don't know. We were told by Edward they were on the floor when he found Jan. I don't think he knows who put them away. Is the bell and sailor's cap and scarf still there?"

"Yes, they're here. The only thing that seems to be missing is the bell rope."

"Who could have put them away?"

"I wouldn't know. It would have to have been someone that came in here right after they took Jan's body away. Let me think a minute. The only people here were Edward, Cheryl and me."

"Well, if you didn't do it and Edward didn't, that only leaves Cheryl. I'll have to call her in the morning."

"Do you want me have her call you?" Florence asked.

"No, that's Ok. We like doing the calling. Sometime a person's response to a question is critical in an investigation. If you find out where the rope went, we'd appreciate you letting us know."

"Well, detectives, I'll let you out. There's a few things I want to catch up on in the office before I leave,"

Walking with them to the theatre exit, she locked the door after they left.

Walking toward the police car, Kadelack asked, "Ben, I wonder where that rope went. I think whoever took it, has something to do with Jan's murder. I'd be willing to bet the knots Edward described on it would probably match the marks on Jan's neck."

"That's the only reason I could see it being missing. Everything Edward described that was on the floor was there," Davis said.

"You know, Ben, Florence seemed pretty annoyed that we were questioning the cast the way we are. It seems as though she's worried more about the play than the discovery of the murderer."

"Well, it's like our job, but there's nothing else we can do short of limiting our interviews to Monday and Tuesday when the theatre's closed. You know that won't fly. Not with everyone breathing down our neck about getting this thing resolved."

"I wonder if it would be a good idea to go to Cheryl's apartment tomorrow morning and ask her" Kadelack said.

"I think that might be the right thing to do instead of calling."

Driving back to headquarters they agreed to meet outside Cheryl's apartment.

***

Meeting the following morning in the lobby of Cheryl's apartment building, Kadelack said, "Well, Ben, I wonder what kind of response we're going to get from Cheryl?"

"Why don't we begin by asking her what time it was when she was in the theatre with Florence? We already know from Edward they came in shortly after the body was removed," Ben said.

"That sounds good," Kadelack replied.

After knocking on the door, Cheryl answered, standing in her robe surprised to see the detectives. Realizing her hair wasn't combed, she quickly ran her hand over her head, and pulled her robe tight to the neck.

"Come in and have a seat," Cheryl said. "You don't mind talking to the back of my head do you? I have to put on the coffee. It's too early in the morning to function without it."

"No, we don't mind. Cheryl, if you can spare the time, we have a few questions to ask you and Carl."

Stretching with a yawn, while looking for the coffee filters, she said, "You can ask me- but you'll have to find Carl to ask him. He never came home after the interview last night."

"Well, some of the cast said you hurried out of the theatre together right after the interview," Kadelack responded.

"Yes, we did, but after we got home, he said he was going out to buy cigarettes and never returned."

They looked at each other bewildered, then at Cheryl.

"Do you have any idea where he went?" Kadelack asked.

Realizing her hair was still uncombed; she ran her hands over it again, trying to look presentable.

"No, I never thought he was anything but happy with our relationship. I can't imagine why he would leave."

"You had a confrontation with Carl at a meeting with Roselyn and Allen. Could you tell us about it?"

Looking surprised they knew about it, she had no alternative but to tell the truth. "Yes, the three of them had a meeting at the Lambertville Tavern to discuss a problem Carl was having."

"What was that problem, do you know?" Kadelack asked.

The aroma of the brewing coffee slowed her response as she got up from the sofa to go to the kitchen.

"You'll have to excuse me. Like I said, I can't function in the morning without that first cup of coffee. Would you gentleman like some?"

"No thanks, we're fine."

Kadelack repeated his question. "The meeting at the Lambertville Tavern- what was Carl's problem?"

Finding a cup in the cabinet and filling it replied, "He was concerned with an insinuation of being somehow connected to Jan being murdered."

Kadelack and Davis glanced at each other with the mutual thought of finally being able to narrow the field of suspects.

"Do you know who made the accusation?" Kadelack asked.

"I think it was Florence. She would be the only other person that would know about his past."

"You obviously know something about his previous marriages. Did you know about him being abusive to his former wives?"

"Yes, I knew that."

"Was he ever abusive while you were living together?"

Pausing, she looked down to turn off the coffee pot.

"No, like I said, I thought we had a great relationship."

"Well, when we interviewed Allen last night, he said you confronted them at the meeting and became very loud about Carl being abusive to you. He told us you were so loud about your verbal assault at Carl, it caught the attention of the other patrons in the bar. That seems to be a contradiction to what you're now telling us. Which is the truth?"

She looked down at her cup.

"Well, officer, no one wants to air their dirty laundry in public. But yes, I was pissed at the meeting by not being invited. Carl and I are supposed to be an item. Wouldn't you be annoyed by having someone else's opinion over the person you're living with?"

"I'd say that was justified," Davis replied. "Is there anything you can tell us?"

"Not really. I guess you'll have to get the fine details from Carl."

Getting up to walk to the door, Officer Davis looked down at a small table and picked up a knotted white braided rope.

"John, look at this!"

"Cheryl, what's this rope for?" Davis asked.

"It's a part of the ships bell from the theatre. How did you get it?" Cheryl asked.

"It was laying right here on this small table. We were looking for this with Florence in the prop room. She said it was missing." Davis replied.

"I saw Carl with it. He came in one day slapping it against his palm. I jokingly asked if he was going to use it on me. We laughed about it, but I thought it was a joke and he brought it back," Cheryl replied.

"Do you mind if we take it?" Davis asked.

"Not at all. Just make sure it winds up back at the theatre. Is there anything else you want to know? I'd really like to get showered and go to breakfast. I don't cook."

"I guess that's the pleasure of being single. That's all we wanted to know. We really want to speak with Carl too. When he returns, tell him to give us a call," Kadelack responded.

"I will."

"Oh! One thing more. What kind of car does Carl have?" Kadelack asked.

"It's a late model maroon Chevy with a cracked passenger side window. Why?"

"I just wanted to know, just in case we have to go looking for him. Thanks for your time."

Walking to the police car, Officer Davis said, "John, we just might have our man. I hope we can bring this thing to a close."

"Look, Ben," Kadelack pointed ahead. "I wonder if that's Carl's car."

Walking over to examine it, they looked it over and peered in the windows on both sides of the car.

"It looks like the car she described. The passenger window's cracked," Kadelack said.

Officer Davis tried the door handle. The driver's side was locked. Detective Kadelack pulled on the passenger door handle, and the door opened.

"Ben, I wonder if she's lying about him being in the apartment," Kadelack asked.

"Do you want to go back and ask?" Davis replied.

"I think we should. If he went for cigarettes as she claimed, he sure as hell didn't walk to get them, especially with the rain we had last night. It's almost a half mile to the nearest store. He has to be in there."

Going back to the apartment they knocked at the door once again. Cheryl answered but seemed annoyed at the second intrusion.

She frustratingly asked, "Did you forget to ask me something else?"

"No, we just wondered if you were telling the truth about Carl not being here. His car is on the parking lot," Davis said.

Surprised, she responded, "It is?"

She went to the window, and looked down at the parking lot to verify the statement.

"Oh! I see why you think I didn't tell you the truth. You can look for yourself. I don't mind."

"Ok, if you say he's not here, we won't dispute it. Do you think Carl went with someone else? Davis asked.

"I don't know. All he said was he had to go for cigarettes. If you find him would you let me know?"

"Yes, we're sorry again for disturbing you."

Chapter 12

Returning to the police car, the detectives heard a radio broadcast calling Detective Kadelack.

Answering it, the broadcaster announced, "Detective, go to the canal on River Road, about a mile south of New Hope on Route 32. The state police are there."

"Can you tell me what it's about? I'm currently on an investigation," Kadelack said.

The broadcaster replied, "A trout fisherman and his son found a body in the canal."

"Ok, we're leaving the apartment complex at River's Edge. We'll be there in about 10 minutes."

Driving South on River Road, a light rain began to fall again. They saw two state police cars parked on the side of the road, just as the broadcaster instructed, about a mile from New Hope.

Exiting their vehicle they were met by a uniformed state trooper. Officer Davis identified himself as a state police detective, and they were escorted across a small footbridge over the canal.

About 100 feet from the footbridge, they met several other uniformed officers standing next to a body lying on the ground under a sheet. When Kadelack pulled it back, it revealed the body of Carl Dunn. He'd been shot in the head. Davis asked the uniformed officer.

"Who discovered the body?"

The uniformed policeman pointed, "That's the man and his son over there."

"Did you take a statement from him?"

"Yes."

While Davis was examining the body, Kadelack identified himself to the man and his son.

"I won't detain you long. I just want to get everything down that happened. What time did you discover the body?"

"Officer Kadelack, my name's Ron Vassor and this is my son Ron Junior. I'm a Philly cop, so I'm familiar with what questions you want to ask. Go ahead."

Kadelack asked the usual- name, address and phone number. He asked Ron to relate the events of finding the body.

"We came to trout fish here," Ron said, "They stock this part of the canal. We got here just before daylight, and I immediately saw the body in the water. I didn't touch anything. I just phoned the police. After they arrived, I helped pull the body up out of the canal."

"That's all for now. If we need you, we know how to get in touch. Thanks," Kadelack said.

Davis turned to Kadelack, pointing to Carl's lifeless body.

"John, there goes our suspect. Where do we go from here?" he asked.

"Well, for a start, let's see if we can match these knots on this rope to the marks on Jan's neck in the photos. I have to go back to headquarters and get a camera. If the medical examiner arrives before I get back, tell him to wait until I can take some pictures," Kadelack said.

"Will do," Davis replied.

When he returned, Dr. Vince Slyker, the medical examiner, was there.

"Hello, Vince. I just want to take a few pictures," Kadelack said.

"Go right ahead," he replied.

After taking photographs of the surrounding area and the canal, he pulled back the sheet and began photographing Carl's remains.

"Vince, did you examine the head wound yet?" Kadelack asked.

"From what I can see, John, it looks like he was shot at close range. I see some powder marks on his hair line at the back of his neck, but I don't see much of an entrance wound. My guess is it had to be a small caliber weapon, like a .22 or even smaller. I'll let you know after the autopsy."

After concluding their work, Ben and John went back to their vehicle.

"John, do you think we should go back and tell Cheryl he's dead?"

Ben asked.

"I think we should. I'm anxious to see what her reaction will be," Kadelack replied.

The light rain falling, while they were at the crime scene, began to come down at a steady pace. After pulling into the parking lot at the apartment complex, Kadelack said, "Well Ben, here goes."

Exiting the vehicle, they dashed across the parking lot to the front door of the apartment building.

Getting to the second floor, Kadelack knocked.

When Cheryl opened the door, she stepped back, speechless for a few moments. She didn't seem angry as she had when they returned after their initial interview.

"I sense you're bringing me bad news, am I correct?" she said.

Looking at Ben, then back at Cheryl Kadelack replied, "I think you better sit down. Yes, I'm bringing you bad news. Carl won't be coming back. He's dead."

Throwing her hands to her face, she began to cry hysterically. Trying to console her, Kadelack put his hand on her shoulder.

"What made you think we were bringing you bad news?" he asked.

"After you left the second time, I was getting ready to step into the shower when a strange feeling overwhelmed me. Call it a premonition or whatever. I knew there was something wrong, definitely wrong. Carl's car wouldn't have been on the lot if he wasn't here."

"Well, since we'll have to interview you about your movements when you last saw him, we might just as well start now."

"Detective Kadelack, how did he die?"

"His body was recovered from the canal about a mile from here by a fisherman and his son. From what we can tell, it appears he'd been shot in the back of the head."

With the words piercing her ears, she lost it completely. Getting up from the couch, she walked nervously around the room, punching her small fist against her open palm.

"I knew something was wrong when he left last night. He said he had to go for cigarettes. But after he left, I found a half pack on the dresser. I called to him as he was going out the door, and I know he had to hear me. I think he made getting the cigarettes an excuse to meet someone."

Punching her open palm once again, she broke down sobbing.

Looking down at his notebook, Kadelack asked. "Could you tell me what time that was?"

"It was about 12:30 last night, just after we got home."

"Do you have any idea who he would be meeting?"

"Not really. Some things he did, he didn't share with me, like the meeting he had with Allen and Roselyn."

"Would you mind if we looked at his personal belongings to see if we can find anything that may give us a clue?"

"No, I don't mind. I'll show you where his closet is. While you're doing that, I'd like to phone Florence and tell her what happened."

"Hold off on calling Florence. We like to do that ourselves."

"Well, she'll have to get Carl's understudy for the play. After Jan's death and now this, she might just close it down altogether."

Looking at his watch, Kadelack said, "She won't make that decision within the next few hours I'm sure. Anyway, I'd like to tell her myself."

"Whatever you say," she replied.

After showing them Carl's closet and dresser drawers, they began rooting through his personal belongings. With nothing of consequence in his dresser drawer, they began searching the clothes in his closet.

Davis took a card from his winter coat pocket.

"John, look at this," Davis said.

"What is it?" Kadelack asked.

"It's a business card with Sam Doherty's name on it."

"Let me see. Is there anything else in the pockets?"

"Just a minute," Davis looked through the inner pocket. Here's another one. It's a business card of Mike Taylor's.

There's a phone number on the back," Davis said.

"Here, let me have the card. I'll dial the number. We'll see who answers it?" Kadelack dialed the number. One ring, two rings, then finally a voice answered.

"Hello, who's calling?" the person on the other end of the line said.

"May I ask if you're the resident?" Kadelack asked.

"Yes, who is this?"

"I'm Detective Kadelack from the New Hope Police Department." He was cut short.

"Yes, detective, is there anything else to report on Jan's death?"

"Is this Peter Austin?" Kadelack asked.

"Yes, it is. What did you learn?" Peter asked.

"We haven't had any further leads. I just thought you'd like to know."

"That's disappointing. I was hoping you had. Thanks anyway for the call."

After hanging up, they thanked Cheryl for being cooperative, then left.

Walking down the corridor, Ben said, "So the number's Peter's. That means it's also Jan's. They were living together."

"That's right, so why would he have her number and Mike Taylor's. Do you think he's the one that hired him?" Kadelack asked.

"I don't know. Something isn't adding up here. They're too many loose ends. "Maybe Sam had Charles and Carl followed?" Davis said.

"I would stick to Sam having Charles followed rather than Carl," Kadelack replied.

Taking the knotted bell rope from his pocket, Kadelack slapped it across his palm. "We still have this. We can try to match up with the pictures of Jan's neck" Kadelack said.

"Well, that's only going to tell us if it was used, which we can almost assure it was, but it isn't going to tell us who was using it. Should we stop at Florence's and tell her what happened?" Davis asked.

"Let's stop at headquarters first. I want to check Jan's photographs."

***

Taking Jan's folder from the file cabinet, they examined the photos.

"Look Ben, it definitely fits the bruise marks. These two knots close together are in line with the two marks on the photo.

I'm going to take this with us to Florence's. It'll be interesting to see what kind of reaction she has when I take it out of my pocket," Kadelack said.

"Good idea," Ben replied.

***

Arriving at the parking lot where Florence lives, Kadelack and Davis saw her coming from the building to her car. Kadelack rolled down the window.

"Good morning, Florence. Can you spare me some time this morning? I'd like to ask you a few questions."

Holding her umbrella over her head while searching her purse for her car keys, she replied, "Let me put these folders in the car. I'll meet you at the front door of the apartment."

She pointed to the building, "That one over there."

After finding a parking space, the detectives met her at the entrance.

"What can I help you with this morning, officer?"

"Would you mind if we use your apartment?" Kadelack asked.

She looked at her watch.

"Is that necessary? I'm sort of squeezed for time this morning," she said.

Just then a tenant passed by.

"Good morning Florence, crappy weather."

"Good morning Steven. It sure is," she replied.

He stood in the doorway briefly, waiting for a break in the rain before making a dash across the parking lot to his vehicle.

In a few minutes another tenant came from an apartment.

"Good morning, Florence."

"Good morning, Sarah."

"If you don't mind Florence, we'd like to conduct this interview in the privacy of your apartment. It seems like you're popular here," Kadelack said.

She hesitated, "Do we really have to? It's a mess. I'm not the greatest housekeeper," she said.

"We don't mind. Whatever it looks like, I assure you we've seen worse."

"Well, I'm self conscious of things like that. I'd rather not," she said.

She seemed to be getting nervous for some reason, and it was becoming apparent she didn't want them in the apartment. Kadelack pushed the issue.

"It won't take long. I assure you it's something I really must tell you."

Reaching in his pocket taking out the rope, his eyes were fixed on Florence's face to see a reaction. Seeing it, she looked surprised.

"That looks like the rope that was missing from the prop room. Where did you get it?" she asked.

Just as Kadelack predicted, her reaction didn't seem like a concern for

R.J. Bonett

something that was misplaced. She had an unjustified reaction, as if it was something incriminating.

She repeated again, "Where did you get that, from the floor of the prop room?"

"I think we better go to your apartment where we can talk," Kadelack said.

Reluctantly, she agreed. She took out her keys and opened the door. A male voice came from another room.

"Back so soon? Did you forget something?"

The voice was familiar. Who was it? She seemed reluctant to reply, but finally said, "Its Detective Kadelack. He wants to ask me a few questions. Have you showered yet?"

The voice hesitated, before finally answering, "Yes."

In a few minutes Peter entered the room, drying his hair with a towel. Wearing a robe he looked surprised to see them standing in the living room.

The detectives looked at each other just as surprised, realizing the phone number Kadelack dialed on the back of the business card at Cheryl's wasn't Peter's apartment. It was Florence's. Kadelack thought, "Cheryl should have surely known it was Florence's phone number when she looked at it. Why didn't she mention it?"

"Officer, what's this all about? Did you forget to tell me something about Jan when you called earlier?" Peter asked.

Not wanting to give away his motives Kadelack responded, "I thought, when I spoke to you earlier, you might have been in your own apartment."

Caught by surprise, he said "I..., I..., came here last night to talk to Florence about my problems and sort of got drunk. She let me spend the night sleeping on the couch rather than drive back home."

Detective Davis noticed the plush pillows on the couch seemed undisturbed.

"Peter, what time did you arrive here last night?" Davis asked.

"About 1 a.m. When you called, I was wondering why you called here to speak to me. You have my phone number at the apartment. Didn't you realize they were different?" Peter asked.

"Actually, Peter, I dialed the number that was on the back of a business card I found in Carl Dunn's coat pocket. I didn't know who's number it was."

"Well, Carl could have told you that."

"I'm sorry to have to tell you this, but Carl's dead."

Florence's face turned pale, and she sat down on the edge of the sofa.

"Dead! How? What happened?"

Peter appeared to be less surprised and asked, "That is a good question, officer. How did he die?"

"He was shot in the head."

Florence quickly asked, "Was it suicide?"

"No, we don't believe so." Not wanting to elaborate more he continued, "He was found about a mile from here. His body was dumped in the canal," Kadelack said.

She seemed to be panic-stricken, but said, "It would have to have been a pretty big person to do that. Carl was a big man."

"We're just beginning to investigate, so I can't elaborate on how it happened. Cheryl said he went out for cigarettes after they got home last night. She thinks he made that excuse as a reason to meet someone. Do you have any idea who that might have been?" Kadelack asked.

Florence looked at Peter, shrugging her shoulders. "I wouldn't have the faintest idea."

Kadelack asked bluntly, "Florence, did you have a relationship with Carl?"

Embarrassed that he asked that kind of a question in front of Peter, she replied, "We had a few meetings, but it was nothing serious. We stopped seeing each other when him and Cheryl began living together. Why?"

"Just asking. Do you think you'll close down the play?"

"I don't know. I'll call his understudy and talk it over with Charles Cohen, the play's financier. He may just want to do that. He wanted to shut it down after Jan was murdered. Is there anything else you wanted to ask me, officer?"

"No, I think that about covers it for now."

As Kadelack and Davis were about to leave, Kadelack turned again asking, "Florence, how well do you know Sam Dougherty?"

Her face became red with embarrassment. "I... I've known Sam ever since I've been associated with the theatre. He was Charles Cohen's partner in some sort of business. For some reason they had a falling out, and Sam never bothered with the theatre after that. Why?"

"Just asking," Kadelack replied.

After closing the door heading for the stairs, Davis asked, "John, what do you make of Peter's reaction when you told them Carl was dead?"

"He sure didn't look or sound like he was surprised- If that's what you mean. He said he didn't get to her apartment till around 1 a.m. The coroner said the time of death was around midnight," kadelack said.

"Florence was right about one thing, though," Davis said.

"What's that?"

Davis looked at Kadelack, "Whoever put him in the canal, had to be pretty strong to do it. Peter doesn't look like he's physically capable of doing it himself. He would have had to have help." Davis said.

"I wonder if we might have missed something at the scene. Let's go back and take another look," Kadelack said.

"Good idea. It stopped raining. Let's go."

***

Getting back to the canal site, everyone else had already gone. Going through the heavy wet grass, they began a closer search for anything they may have missed. Davis widened his search, while Kadelack concentrated on the immediate area of the path that would have been taken to put the body where it was discovered.

Davis stopped about 50 feet off the path and called out, "John, come over here. Look at this."

Kadelack joined him, and Davis pointed to a wet blood-soaked towel lying on the ground.

"Does this look familiar?" Davis asked.

Stooping down to get a better look without touching it he looked up at Davis.

"Are you thinking what I'm thinking?"

"Yes, it's the same type of plush towel Peter was drying his hair with. The same color too. I'll get an evidence bag from the car," Kadelack said.

After returning, Davis picked up a stick lying on the ground. Carefully using it to pick up the towel, they looked it over as Detective Kadelack slowly lowered it into the evidence bag.

"John, wait!"

"What's wrong?"

"Do you notice how the blood stains look? If it's connected to Carl's death, which I believe we'll discover it is, it appears that it was used to wrap around his head, probably trying to prevent the blood from getting on anything," Davis said as he pointed with his finger. "See, the stains are circular and larger at one end, getting gradually smaller as it was wrapped around. I think we should go back to Florence's and ask a few more questions," Davis said.

Looking around a little more, Kadelack discovered a book of matches with the logo of the Lambertville Tavern on it.

After putting it in a small evidence bag, he said, "Ben, I don't know whether this is part of the investigation, but I'm taking it too. You're right. I think we should stop back at Florence's on the way to the police station. I don't know whether we'll see her. She was about to leave when we pulled up earlier. Remember?"

"Yes. But maybe Peter is still there. We can ask him a few things."

Confident they hadn't missed anything, they left.

Pulling into the parking lot, they saw Florence getting ready to get in her car again.

"Florence, excuse me. I..." Davis said.

Cutting him off short, she glanced at her watch.

"Look, Detective. I'm already late with a 10 o'clock appointment. Whatever you have to ask, couldn't it wait until later? After the show this afternoon, I can come to the police station for another interview."

As Florence was about to get into her car, Kadelack said, "I guess you had the opportunity to speak to Charles Cohen. He must have decided the play should continue, right?"

"That's right, so if you'll excuse me," Florence said.

Before she could get in, a neighbor tenant walked by.

"Hi, Florence. For two people that keep late hours, you and Peter get up pretty early."

Not responding to the neighbor's statement as if she didn't hear her, she got in the car and drove away.

"Ben, did you hear that woman?" Kadelack asked.

"Yes, I did. I wonder what time she saw them last night."

Following the woman to the lobby, the detectives stopped her at the elevator showing their identification.

"Excuse me, ma'am. I'm Detective Kadelack and this is Detective Ben Davis from the state police. Do you mind if we ask you a few questions?"

As she struggled with her grocery bags, she replied, "No, officer, I don't mind. Why don't you come to my apartment? These bags are getting heavy."

"I'm sorry, ma'am. Here, let me help," Davis said. He took one and Kadelack took the other. Following her to the apartment, Kadelack asked, "Can I ask your name?"

"I'm sorry, officer. I'm Carol Winslow."

"We heard you mention to Florence about coming in late last night. Do you remember what time that was?"

Just before the detectives stepped into Carol's apartment, Peter came out of Florence's apartment.

"Hello, Peter. I just saw Florence leaving. She must have a lot on her mind. She didn't even acknowledge me," Carol said.

Not sure how to answer, he began coming in their direction, addressing the detectives. "Officers, did you want to ask me anymore questions? If you do, I'm about to leave. I can wait around or join you in Carol's apartment," Peter said.

Kadelack responded, "Not right now, Peter. Maybe later."

Hesitating, he didn't want it to appear obvious that he wanted to know what the conversation with Carol was going to be about. He turned, then, slowly walked toward the elevator. Looking back over his shoulder, he said, "Whenever you want me, you know where I'll be."

Davis replied, "At the theatre, right? Florence just told us it's continuing."

"I know. She phoned Charles from her apartment. Well, see you later," Peter said.

Entering the apartment the detectives heard an alarm from another room.

Carol said, "Would you put the grocery bags on the kitchen table? I must have forgotten to turn off my alarm clock this morning before I went out. Can I make you some coffee?"

"No thanks ma'am. Do you remember what time Florence came in this morning?" Kadelack asked.

"Yes, it was about 2 a.m. In fact, I know it was 2 a.m. I was just finishing a book I was reading. I was near the end of a mystery, and wanted to know who the murderer was before I went to bed. I'm an avid reader. When I was finished, I went to the window to see if it was still raining, that's when I saw them getting out of Florence's car."

Davis and Kadelack looked at each other, realizing Peter was lying about the time he came in.

"Officer, Is there a certain reason for asking?" Carol asked.

Looking at her, not wanting to divulge too much, the detectives remained silent.

"You said them. I take it, it was Peter and Florence?"

"Yes," Carol replied.

Still not divulging an answer to her question, Davis replied, "Just asking, ma'am. That's all we wanted to know. If we do have any more questions, we'll be in touch."

After leaving the apartment, Davis said, "I wonder why they didn't tell us they were out together? I think we should get that towel to the lab and see if the blood type matches Carl's."

"I think you're right. I wonder if there's anything visible as far as a blood stain in Florence's car? Why don't we drive by the theatre and see if her car is there?" Kadelack asked.

"That's what I was thinking," Davis said.

Chapter 13

Arriving at the lab, Kadelack and Davis entered the office of the medical examiner.

Kadelack asked, "Dr. Slyker, I know it's only been a few hours since you brought Carl Dunn's body in, but have you had a chance to examine it?"

"I've just begun and only did a preliminary. Here's the clothing that was removed."

"Have you by chance had an opportunity to examine the bullet wound?" Davis asked.

"Yes, externally. It was fired at almost point blank range, and there were traces of powder burns around the entrance of the skull under his hair. There's no exit wound, so my assumption is it had to be a small caliber weapon, as I mentioned to you at the scene. I'll know more after a complete autopsy."

"Did you get an opportunity to ascertain a blood type?" Davis asked, "We went back to the scene and found a blood-soaked towel near where the body was recovered. I'm really interested if it's the same."

"The lab technician was notified," Dr. Slyker said, glancing up at the wall clock.

"He should be here at any time. I'll tell him to do that first."

"Thank you, Dr. Slyker. We have a few other things we want to check on. Could you call the police department office after you have your findings?" Davis asked.

"Yes, I'll relay your message," Dr. Slyker said.

Getting back to the car, Kadelack said, "Why don't we go by the theatre parking lot and see if there's anything visible in Florence's car?"

"Do you think we should obtain a warrant first?" Davis asked.

"No. Not at this point. If we see something, then we'll get a warrant."

Driving by the local car wash, Davis said, "John, look. Isn't that Florence?"

"Yes it is, but I don't see her car. Why don't we park and watch. It's probably already in the washing process," Kadelack said.

Pulling into a parking space close by, to their surprise, she got into a different vehicle other than her own. It was a maroon-colored Lincoln sedan.

Kadelack said, "That looks like Sam's car. I wonder why she's driving it? She left her apartment complex in her own?"

"Let's follow her to see where she goes," Davis said.

They waited until she pulled away then followed at a safe distance. She drove south on Rt. 32, then stopped near the site of where Carl's body was found. She looked around the spot where the towel was recovered.

Apparently not finding what she was looking for, got back in the car and drove further south until she reached a large home with meticulously manicured grounds. The name on the mail box at the entrance read, S. Dougherty.

The detectives saw Sam come from the house and get into the driver's seat then pull away. They followed them back to the theatre parking lot where Florence got out, and leaned on the open window of the passenger side talking to Sam. After several minutes, she walked toward the theatre. Looking back, she waved as the Lincoln pulled away.

Kadelack said, "Look, there's Florence's car over there. Let's wait until after she gets in the theatre and take a look."

Davis replied, "If she was at the car wash with Sam's car, I would suspect it might have had something to do with last night."

"You're probably right, but let's take a look anyway," Kadelack said.

Pulling up next to the car, they got out and looked in the windows.

Davis remarked after a brief examination.

"I don't see anything, do you?"

"No, at least we can rule that theory out," Kadelack replied.

"Let's go back to the crime site and see if there's anything we might have missed. Do you think she might have lost something at the scene?" Davis asked.

"There's only one way to find out. Let's go back."

On the way to the scene, they received a radio call from the dispatcher. He informed them that the medical examiner's office called with an ID on Carl's blood type. It was O negative, the same blood type on the towel found at the scene.

"John, that's a rare blood type isn't it?"

"I don't know how rare, but it's a blood type they call a universal donor. The people that have it can donate to any blood type."

Pulling up to the scene, they got out and began going over the ground where the wet grass was disturbed by Florence. Back and forth they went, straining their eyes for any clue as to what she may have been looking for.

Kadelack suddenly stopped.

"Hey look what I found," he said.

"What is it?"

Davis joined him and they focused on a broken watch band.

Picking it up, they examined it.

"By the looks of it, I'd say it's probably a part of a gold band from an expensive wristwatch. I think it might be a Rolex, or something just as expensive," Kadelack said.

"It doesn't look like it's been here very long. It's not even dirty," Davis replied.

"Well, it's not a woman's watch. Do you think we should confront her with it?"

"Yes, I think it's time to interview Florence."

On the way back to the theatre, they talked about the strategy they would employ asking her questions.

"I think we should start by asking her about the difference in the time she said Peter came in, and the time the neighbor mentioned. We can also ask why she didn't tell us they came in together, rather than give us the impression she was home when he came in," Kadelack said.

"Did you want to mention seeing her at the car wash then driving to the crime scene?" Davis asked.

"Let's not divulge too much right now. I don't want her to know we followed her there- then followed her to Sam's.

We could get her to come to police headquarters for the interview. I don't want her to call Sam and give them a chance to make up a story. We can't allow them to know they're both being summoned. Depending on what they say will determine whether we should get a warrant to search Sam's car."

"That sounds good. Why don't we stop by the theatre? It's on the way back to the medical examiner's office. Hopefully he had time to examine the bullet wound."

Entering the theatre, they saw the cast gathered outside the main office. Florence was informing them of Carl's death. Whispers among them were interrupted by Roselyn.

"Florence, Is the play going to be cancelled?" she asked.

"No, I spoke to Charles this morning, and he said it should continue for awhile using Carl's understudy. I spoke to the understudy this morning. He's ready to fill in. That's all I have so far, but I suspect we'll be seeing the detectives for more interviews," Florence said.

Seeing them coming toward the cast, she added, "Talk about timing. Here they are now."

Kadelack remarked, "We won't tie you up very long. It's a matter of routine. We'd like to know the last time you saw Carl alive. If you don't mind, Florence, we'd like to use your office for the interviews. If the cast could come up one at a time, it shouldn't take very long."

"Go right ahead. Should I call Charles and ask him to be here?" she asked.

"No, that's alright. Has anyone seen Peter?" Kadelack asked.

No one responded for a few moments until Roselyn replied, "I saw him earlier when he was talking to you, Florence."

Florence was clearly embarrassed that Roselyn gave Kadelack that information, but didn't comment.

After looking over the cast, making sure he wasn't there, Kadelack said, "Let's get these interviews done. We can talk to Mr. Cohen and Peter later. In no certain order, would you come up to the office one at a time?"

Interviewing each one, the conclusions were all the same. No one saw Carl after the last performance.

The detectives waited for Florence to come in. Ten minutes went by, then 15 minutes. Finally, Kadelack opened the door and called down to Allen.

"That's it for the cast. Would you ask Florence to come up," Kadelack asked.

After looking around, Allen replied. "I think she left the theatre a few minutes after you began the interviews."

Looking around to be sure she'd gone, Allen looked up, repeating himself, "Yes, she left."

Wondering why she left before being interviewed, the detectives came down from the office. Putting on his coat, Kadelack asked, "Allen, when she returns, give her my card. Have her call me at this number."

"Okay, are you finished with us?"

"Yes, for now. We'll let you know if there's anything else."

Leaving the theatre, Kadelack and Davis saw Florence pulling into the parking lot. When she got out of the car, Kadelack asked, "Where did you get to?"

"I didn't think you wanted to interview me again since we already had our talk this morning. Is there something else you wanted to ask?" she said.

"Yes, I'd like you to come to headquarters and give me a formal statement. If at all possible, could it be Monday morning at, let's say 10 a.m.?"

"That's not a problem. We don't have a show Monday," she replied.

"I'll see you then," Kadelack said.

After she went back into the theatre, Davis asked, "Do you think she left to contact Sam about the interviews here this morning?"

"I don't know. We'll find out on Monday. When we interview her, I'll confront her with us seeing her with Sam's car and being at the crime scene. If we do it separately when we interview Sam, they may just trip each other up."

Satisfied with their strategy for the interviews, they headed for the medical examiner's office. Entering the room they observed the naked body of Carl with the M.E. closely examining the head wound.

"Dr. Slyker, is there anything else you can tell us about the head wound?" Kadelack asked.

"Detective, just as I mentioned before, the bullet was fired from almost a point-blank range. The weapon must have been pointed in the upward position. There's something else I'd like to point out."

"What's that, doctor?" Kadelack asked.

"Look at the right forearm. It's a stab wound that's several days old, but it looks pretty deep. I would say this wasn't an accident," Dr. Slyker said.

After examining it, Kadelack picked up a small metal tray lying next to the examination tools.

"Is this the bullet you retrieved? There's not much damage to it. It looks like a .22 short."

"It is, but Doctor Slyker, if it was fired at point blank range, why didn't it go through the skull instead of remaining inside?"Davis asked.

Putting down the autopsy instrument he was using, he looked up and said, "It was fired in an upward position, and the path of the bullet was slowed on entry by penetrating the skull, then followed the inside curvature to the point where it stopped. The deceased has what's commonly referred to as a double skull."

"What's that?" Davis asked.

"It's an anomaly where the skull bone is abnormally thicker than the normal thickness, common in some people. That's one of the reasons it remained inside the skull. Had it been fired straight, more than likely it would have gone through the skull, damaging the eyes, nostrils, or sinus area, before exiting."

"Then, either the person was a lot shorter than the deceased, or the deceased was bent forward for that to have happened?" Davis stated.

"That would be my theory. The path of the bullet favored the center of the skull," Dr. Slyker confirmed.

Kadelack remarked to Davis, "Seeing Florence at the car wash, it could have been done by a person sitting behind the deceased if it took place in a car. By Carl's height, he may have been sitting in one of the front seats. My guess, it would have been the passenger side. If it was, then we're dealing with 3 people that were there at the time. Carol Winslow said Florence and Peter came in together at around 2 a.m. instead of 1 a.m. as they told us. Let's not forget the blood-soaked towel we found at the scene, looks to be the same pattern as the one Peter was drying with, when he came into the living room at Florence's."

"I know, but like I said, I think we should leave questioning Florence go until Monday. There's no point in doing it now. Let her have a few days where she thinks the pressures off, then we'll have a better chance to ask about the discrepancy with the time her and Peter came home, as well as the rest of what we know about her movements after the car wash," Davis said.

Taking the bullet as evidence, they returned to police headquarters.

As the detectives entered the building, the desk sergeant said, "Detective Kadelack, there's a person waiting in your office."

"Who is it?"

"He said his name is Charles Cohen. Are you expecting him?"

Looking at Davis, he replied, "No, not expecting him, but we did want to interview him. Thanks."

Kadelack addressed Davis. "Maybe that's why Florence left the theatre. She might have phoned him about the interviews."

"That's a good possibility too. I guess we'll find out," Davis replied.

When they entered the office, Charles was seated next to a desk, and then stood up.

With nervousness in his voice, Charles asked, "Detective Kadelack, Florence phoned me about the interviews at the theatre. Is there something you wanted to ask me?"

"Yes, I guess Florence already told you Carl Dunn's dead."

He stood up surprised at his statement, and became pale. His nervousness took on the expression of fright in his face, and he sat back down.

With his arm resting on the desk he began tapping nervously with his fingers.

"Dead! Who killed him?" Charles asked.

"Unless Florence already told you, how do you know he was murdered?"

"She mentioned it. But there's nothing I can add to it."

"When was the last time you saw Carl alive?" Kadelack asked.

"I saw him, Florence, Cheryl and Peter at the Lambertville Tavern late last night."

"Can you tell us approximately what time that was?"

Looking more nervous, he said, "I can tell you exactly. It was 11:30. That's about a half hour after the play ended. Sometimes the players go there for a drink and some social life."

"What else did you observe?"

"I didn't feel like joining them, so I sat at the bar. I saw Carl and Cheryl leave about 15 minutes later."

"Did Florence and Peter stay?"

"Yes, they joined me at the bar."

"Do you remember what was said?"

"Yes, we talked about the play and when I thought it should end. It had been going pretty successfully since last November. Generally, the life of a play like that wanes in about six to nine months."

Kadelack remarked, "Did Peter say anything in particular that you can remember?"

"No, nothing out of the ordinary; Peter's not a drinker by any sense of the word. I'd been in his company before. It doesn't take too many drinks before he gets plastered. I think he was still distraught over Jan's death. From what I understand, they were going to get married."

"Did Florence say anything out of the ordinary?"

"No, she seemed a little out of sorts that Peter was getting drunk, that's about all."

"What was she saying?"

"She kept asking Peter to come with her."

"Did he leave with her?"

"No, she was getting more perturbed at his insistence on staying. She probably drove him there. He doesn't own a car of his own as far as I know. He was using Jan's car. Frustrated that he wouldn't leave, she finally left by herself."

"Do you know what time that was?"

"That was close to midnight."

"Are you positive of the time?"

"Yes, I was supposed to meet a young lady there. I looked at my watch. She was already late by a half hour. I thought the downpour may have been keeping her."

"Did you remain at the bar, or did you leave?"

"Like I said, I was waiting for someone."

"What was Peter doing?"

"By that time he was really smashed, so I called Florence to see if she could give him a ride home. I couldn't get through to her. She was either out or didn't want to answer the phone. She was really pissed when she left. She can be pretty demanding at times."

"I take it you know that on a personal level and not just professionally?"

Looking up embarrassed, he replied, "Yes, I know that personally. We had a relationship for awhile, if that's what you're referring to."

"Did the woman you were supposed to meet ever show up?"

"No, either she was held up by the storm, or she..." He hesitated.

"She what?" Kadelack asked.

Charles looked down at the floor, not wanting to answer.

Davis, listening intently to the interview asked, "Can you give us the name of the girl? We'd like to speak to her."

Looking up at him, Charles said, "I'd rather not get her involved. She's married."

"What time did you leave the bar?"

"I stayed until almost closing. I was going to take Peter with me, but as I was walking him to the door, Florence came in.

I helped get him to her car then she drove away."

"What time was that?"

"Like I said, the bar was about to close early for a lack of customers. I'd say it was about 1:45."

"Did you notice anything out of the ordinary about Florence?"

"She seemed very nervous, and I asked her why she came back to the bar."

"What did she say?"

"She said she went by Jan's apartment to check on Peter, but when she saw he wasn't there, she figured he was still with me at the bar. She knew he was still upset about Jan's death."

"That's about all the questions we have right now, you can go."

Walking him to the door, Davis fired another quick question.

"How long after Jan's death was it before Peter took up a relationship with Florence?"

"That's something I don't know. If he did, it couldn't have been very long."

Closing the door behind him, Davis said to Kadelack, "Now we know

Florence wasn't out with Peter all evening. She must have just brought him back to her apartment after leaving the bar. I wonder where she was for an hour and a half, before the neighbor saw them come home? Without physical evidence, there's no way we can tie her to the murder. The only thing we know is she was missing for an hour and a half. We can't even connect her being with Sam, unless we get a warrant for his car and find something. At that, there isn't any probable cause. The only way would be the interview with Florence and try tripping her up on the time she left the bar, and the time she returned to pick up Peter?" Kadelack said.

"I wonder how she knew he was still at the bar."

"That's one of the questions we should ask."

Chapter 14

During the weekend, Detective Kadelack passed through the parking lot at the theatre several times on a chance he may see something unusual. Several passes on Saturday didn't reveal anything out of the ordinary.

Passing through just before Sunday's performance, he saw what looked like Sam Doherty's maroon-colored Lincoln pulling into the lot and park by the theatre side door. He thought, was it his, or was it the same make and color of someone else's? Pulling into a blank parking space, Kadelack turned off the motor to watch.

Within a few minutes, the side door of the theatre opened slightly. After a few moments Florence exited, heading for the maroon Lincoln. The passenger door was opened from the driver side and she got in.

About five minutes later, the side door opened again. This time Cheryl came out and headed for the Lincoln. She banged on the passenger's side window, yelling at Florence.

Kadelack rolled down his window to try hearing the conversation, but couldn't. Whatever it was, it was obvious it wasn't about the play.

After what appeared to be a few minutes of Cheryl ranting and waving her fist, Florence stepped from the car. After saying a few words to the driver, Florence closed the passenger door then headed toward the theatre. Cheryl seemed to be in hot pursuit, continuing her verbal assault until they were inside. The Lincoln slowly pulled away exiting the parking lot.

Noting the time, Kadelack remained a few minutes, then left. He thought to himself, I wonder what that was all about. Whatever it was, it gives me something to interject when I interview Florence tomorrow morning.

***

At 8:00 the next morning, Ben entered the police station. Opening the door to Kadelack's office, he was met with a smile.

Pouring a cup of coffee, Kadelack asked, "Ben, care to join me?"

"Sure, smells good. Why the grin, did something happen over the weekend I should know about?"

"You won't believe what I saw. I drove by the theatre several times over the weekend on a chance I might see something. Sunday, before the matinee began, I saw Sam's Lincoln drive in the parking lot, and backed into a space where I could see what he was going to do," Kadelack explained.

Pausing for a moment, he handed Davis a cup of coffee, then smiled again.

"Well, stop with the suspense. What happened?"

Smiling again, Kadelack said, "In a few minutes Florence came out the side door of the theatre and got in the car. About five minutes later, Cheryl came out the door and went straight to the Lincoln. She started banging on the passenger side and yelling."

"What was she yelling?"

"I couldn't make out what was being said. I was too far away. In a few minutes, Florence exited the car and headed for the theatre. Cheryl looked like she was still pissed for whatever reason, and continued blasting her back to the theatre."

"What do you think that was about?"

After taking a few sips of the hot coffee, he looked up.

"I don't know, but I think we have a shocker question when Florence comes in for the interview at 10:00."

"Actually we have two shocker questions," Davis said. "I was thinking about asking her about driving Sam's car to the car wash, then going back to where we retrieved the towel. It looks like this whole thing's coming to a head."

Looking up at the clock, Kadelack said, "It's only a little past 8:00. I wonder, is it a better idea to catch her off guard and go to her apartment?"

"That's a good idea," Davis replied.

After finishing the coffee, they left.

Getting to her apartment, Kadelack was about to knock when the door suddenly opened. Florence, who was about to leave, was surprised to see them.

Davis looked at his watch. It was 8:45.

"If you're leaving for the interview, you're kind of early," Davis said.

"No, detective. I was going to stop for coffee and a little breakfast on Main Street, before I got there," Florence said.

"Well, we can save you the trouble. We thought we would interview you here. You don't mind, do you?"

Shaken by his request, she fumbled for words.

"Ah, no, I don't mind. Why don't you have a seat in the living room? I'd like to put on coffee first. Would you like some?"

She headed for the kitchen.

"I'd like a cup," Davis replied.

As Davis looked around the room before sitting down, his eyes caught something on an end table next to the couch where Kadelack was sitting. Tapping Kadelack on the arm without speaking, he pointed to a wrist watch with a broken band. Kadelack picked it up to examine and noticed a few links missing. It was the same type of band as the piece recovered near the crime scene. Pointing to the few missing links, he was about to put it down when Florence entered the room.

Noticing him looking at the watch, she nervously said, "That belongs to Peter. He left it here the other night when he stayed over. He said he didn't know how it got broken and asked me to take it to the watch repair on Main Street. I was going to do that this morning too. I'm glad you picked it up. I forgot all about it. Ok, now where do we begin this interview?"

Kadelack began by opening his note book asking, "Do you remember-You told us Peter came in around midnight the night he stayed over."

She paused for a moment. "Yes, I remember. He was drunk out of his mind."

"You never mentioned to us that you were out with him. You gave us the impression that you were already here," Kadelack said.

Her face became red with embarrassment. She was caught completely off guard. Getting up from the chair, she tried concealing her reaction. "I think that coffee's about done. Let me get you some, cream and sugar?"

"Black, if you don't mind," Davis replied.

Pointing at Kadelack, "And you?"

"Same."

Returning to the living room with the tray, she nervously answered the question.

"I didn't think I gave you that impression. Is it important?"

Kadelack looked over his notebook.

"I think it is. Your neighbor, Carol Winslow, said she saw you and Peter come in together."

Florence replied as if she was exonerated. "Well, there you go. She even told you."

He looked at his note book once again.

"Yes, but you said it was close to midnight, and your neighbor said it was 2 o'clock, two o'clock precisely. She told us she had just finished reading a book, and went to the window to see if it was still raining."

Attempting to put her cup on the coffee table, she miscalculated, spilling some.

"I'm sorry. I guess I didn't remember," she said.

"Were you and Peter out drinking or partying all evening?"

She looked at them, not knowing how to answer.

Noticing her nervousness, Kadelack didn't want to disclose any more than necessary without giving her the opportunity to have legal counsel.

"Florence, I think that's all we'd like to ask you right now. If you could come into the office this afternoon about 2:00, we can finish."

Trying to pass off her nervousness, she jokingly replied, "Shall I bring a lawyer?"

He looked her straight in the eye, and with seriousness in his voice, replied, "Yes, I think that would be a good idea."

Florence realized he wasn't impressed by her remark. Her facial expression went blank. No embarrassment, just a blank look of uncertainty.

Leaving the apartment, Davis asked, "Do you think we should have just brought her in?"

"No, this gives her time to think up a story that we'll be able to refute. I'm sure she doesn't realize we already have a statement from Charles as to where Peter was at the time. Couple that, with seeing her with Sam's car at the carwash, I'm almost sure she'll break. It'll be enough pressure."

"Do you think we should bring in Sam Dougherty?"

"I think we should bring him in after we get her statement," Kadelack said.

"You said you saw Cheryl confronting her in the parking lot. Should we stop at Cheryl's apartment and ask her a few questions?"

"At this point, neither Florence, or Cheryl, know I saw them arguing. Let's just leave it until we record what Florence has to say. If there's anything that connects Cheryl to Carl's death, it can be played back to her. I think that's what will break this thing wide open."

Returning to the office, they saw Charles waiting in the lobby.

"You're not scheduled for an interview. Is there something else you want to tell us?" Davis asked.

"Just that I stopped by the boarding house where Roselyn and Allen live to ask them if they knew anything about the relationship between Cheryl and Carl."

"And did they?" Kadelack replied.

"Probably nothing more than you already know."

"Okay, what do you think we know?"

"Only that they suspected Carl was the one that beat Jan on New Year's Eve. Didn't either one of them tell you?" Charles asked.

"No, this is the first time we're hearing it. Did Sam Dougherty know that?"

"I don't think he did until after he confronted me with it in my driveway after it happened. I don't know how he found out, but he must have believed me, and put two and two together. It could have been from Roselyn mentioning Carl being pushy about trying to start a relationship with her. I know Florence knew it. Maybe she mentioned it to her."

"We never knew Roselyn had a problem with Carl, thanks for the info."

"Do you know anyone outside the theatre that would've wanted him dead?"

Charles turned before walking out the door.

"With his attitude toward women, probably quite a few. I know he had a bad situation with the person he was married to. From what I heard from Cheryl, that's how he wound up in this area."

After Charles left, Kadelack picked up the phone dialing Cheryl's number. Getting a busy signal, he cradled the phone.

"Who were you calling?" Ben asked.

"I dialed Cheryl's number, but the line's busy. I'll try again in a few minutes."

New Hope

"Are you going to bring her in for an interview?"

"I'm going to ask if she can stop by around 11:00. She may be able to tell us more about Carl," Kadelack said. After dialing her number again, it was picked up on the second ring. Before he had a chance to speak, a voice he took to be Cheryl's said, "Sam, is Florence being interviewed today?"

Kadelack recognizing the voice replied, "Cheryl, this isn't Sam."

Recognizing his voice, she fell silent for a few moments.

"Oh, Detective Kadelack, it's you. Is there something you wanted to ask?" she said.

"Yes, I was wondering if you could come to the office this morning around 11:00. I just have a few things I'd like to clear up about Carl's past."

"Could you ask me over the phone? I'm really busy today."

Being stern with his request, he lied, "I think it's to your benefit."

A few more moments passed before she answered, "Ok, I'll try to get finished with my errands as quickly as possible. I'll be there."

Hanging up the phone, Davis asked, "What did she say?"

Kadelack held up his index finger motioning for him to wait a second. He redialed Cheryl's number, and as he suspected, the phone line was busy. She must have been talking to Sam, but what about?

Ben asked again, "What's that all about?"

"When I dialed her number the first time, the line was busy. When I got through the second time, before I spoke, she said excitedly, "Sam, is Florence being interviewed today?" After I hung up, I redialed her number. As I suspected, her phone line was busy. I'd lay odds 10 to 1 that she called Sam."

With a smile on his face, Ben clapped his hands together then replied, "Hot diggity dam! I think we're going to solve this within the next few days."

Smiling, Kadelack leaned back in his chair, clasping his hands together behind his head too, he replied, "I think you're right, but we lack one thing."

"What's that?"

"A motive, I wonder if anyone in the play knows more about why he wound up dead. Why don't we talk to Roselyn? She was the one that had the confrontation with him. Let's try and interview her and Allen later today. I have her address. Her, and Allen are living in the same boarding

143

house. I'll give her a call."

Thumbing through the interviews that were taken, he found the phone number of the boarding house. Dialing the number, it rang quite a few times. Just as he was about to hang up, he heard a female voice,

"Hello, Ethel's Boarding House. How may I help you?"

"I'm Detective Kadelack, New Hope Police Department. Is this Ethel?"

"Yes, young man. I remember you when you came here on New Year's Eve to talk to Roselyn and Allen about the girl that was beat up."

"That's right. You have a good memory."

"I read in the paper she was killed. Did you find the murderer yet?"

"Unfortunately, not yet, but we hope to soon. Is Roselyn or Allen there?"

"No, you just missed them by 5 minutes."

"Do you know if they're out for the day?"

With a chuckle she replied, "With those two love birds, that's hard to tell. Do you want me to give them a message?"

"Please. If you could have one of them call, I'd appreciate it."

"Wait just a second while I get a pencil and paper."

After giving her the number, Kadelack cradled the phone.

Davis asked, "I guess they weren't there?"

"No, I left the number. I did learn though, Allen and Roselyn are an item. She called them 'Love birds.'"

"I assumed as much from the interviews we had with them."

Within the hour, Cheryl stood in the open doorway to the office, gently knocking.

Looking up from examining the paperwork on the case, Kadelack said, "Come in, please. Have a seat here next to my desk."

In a half-hearted attempt to be funny, Cheryl jokingly said, "I'm by myself this morning. My attorney, Perry Mason, was busy shooting a TV show."

Kadelack looked over his shoulder at Davis and smiled.

"I won't keep you very long, if you'll just bare with me."

She adjusted herself in the chair, and Kadelack could see she was a little nervous.

"Tell me again. What took place the evening you last saw Carl alive?" he asked.

144

Seemingly trying to remember what they did that evening she began to retrace their steps.

"By the time we handed in our garments for the play, it was about 10:45. We spoke to Allen and Roselyn for a few moments outside of the wardrobe room then left the theatre. We went to the Lambertville Tavern with Peter and Florence then went back to the apartment. That's about all."

Looking down at his notes Kadelack said, "You said after you got to the apartment, Carl said he had to go back out for cigarettes. You told me you wondered why he wanted to go back out that late in all that rain. There was a half pack of cigarettes on the dresser in the bedroom. Is that the last time you saw him?"

"Yes."

"Then I take it that it was just an excuse to meet someone, and he didn't want you to know who?"

She replied as an after-thought, "Maybe not. I don't remember telling him about the cigarettes in the bedroom. I might have seen them after he left. I don't remember."

She paused for a moment, realizing she might not have understood the depth of his question, and snapped back, "Are you suggesting he may have been seeing someone else, perhaps another woman?"

"No, I'm just trying to understand if there's something we haven't uncovered, but while we're on the subject, did he ever give you a reason to suspect him of seeing another woman?"

Appearing to be irritated at the suggestion she responded defensively, "No, we had a pretty good relationship."

"How long have you two been living together?"

"Several months."

"In your time living together, I'm sure he must have mentioned his past. Do you know anything about it?"

Looking down at the floor she appeared to be gathering her thoughts of how much she should expose of his marital history.

"He only told me he had a rough marriage and..." She stopped short of a complete answer.

Kaedelack was waiting for her to complete the statement, and looked up. "Go on. He had a rough marriage and what?"

Realizing he was pushing for more information, she replied, "That's about all I can tell you."

"Ok. If you can think of anything else, let us know."

Just as she was getting up, Detective Davis asked, "When we were in your apartment looking through Carl's coat, we found a phone number. You never told us it was Florence's. You should have known that from the start. I'm sure you've called her plenty of times in your association with her at the theatre."

She seemed embarrassed and temporarily fumbled for words. "I... I guess I was upset finding out Carl was dead. Is that all you wanted to know?" Cheryl asked.

"For right now, yes. If you can think of anything else, give us a call," Davis said.

Looking back at Kadelack before exiting the room, she replied, "I will."

Ten minutes after she left, the phone rang.

"Hello, Detective John Kadelack speaking. How may I help you?"

"Detective, this is Allen Simpson. You called here asking to speak with Roselyn and I. What's it about?"

Looking at the clock on the wall, Kadelack replied, "I'd like to interview you about a few things you might be able to clear up. What would be a good time for you?"

"Just a minute."

Kadelack could hear a muffled question from Allen to Roselyn.

'It's Detective Kadelack. He wants to get together with us today. Do you have a time in mind?'

He could hear her answer 'Any time is fine with me. Why not do it now?'

Hearing what she said, before Allen could relay the message, Kadelack replied, "How about 2:00 this afternoon."

With a light chuckle, Allen said, "That's fine. Should we come to your office?"

"Yes, if you would."

"Ok, we'll see you then."

After hanging up the phone, Roselyn asked, "Did he say what it was about?"

"No, but I'm sure it has something to do with how much we know about Carl. We'll just have to wait and see," Allen said.

Ethel, passing Allen and Roselyn in the hall, shook her head in disgust, "Someone should write a play based on the events of the past several months. What shall we call it, the theatre murders?"

Roselyn giving her a surprised look, replying, "Ethel, that's not a bad idea."

They left for the police station and at 2 p.m., they knocked at the door of Kadelack's office.

"Come in. Please, have a seat. I'll be with you in a moment," Kadelack said.

Hanging up the phone he asked, "I hope I'm not interrupting your day off?"

Roselyn replied, "Not really. We had planned to go to the city for a few days, but the weather's kind of blah." She smiled at Allen. "Maybe it'll be better next week."

"Well, I'm glad you took the time to come in. How well do you, or rather I should say, what do you know about the relationship between Carl and Cheryl? Is it as amicable as Cheryl claims it was?"

Looking at each other with raised eyebrows, they said almost simultaneously, "No."

Davis looked at them then at Kadelack asked, "You mean there was a problem between them?"

"Yes, I think Carl wanted to end the relationship a while back," Roselyn replied.

"How do you know that?" he asked.

"He wanted to meet with us privately to talk about Florence having some suspicion he was responsible for Jan's death," Allen replied.

Allen's statement exposed more about a relationship between Carl and Florence, and brought full attention from Davis and Kadelack.

"How does Cheryl fit in here?" Davis asked.

"When we met at the Lambertville Tavern after the last performance, Cheryl walked in on us. She was loud about not being invited to the meeting, and began a triad against Carl that as we say in the theatre,

'Would have brought down the house.' She went on and on, saying things that I'm sure were only to embarrass him."

"Things like what? Do you remember?"

"Oh, about how she pays the bills, and how abusive he is when they have sex. Things that were only meant to embarrass him. Mean, vindictive statements," Allen said.

Kadelack looked at him for a few moments before replying, "And this was said before she knew what the meeting with you was about?"

"Yes, after she left, he voiced his concern about her being so dominant in their relationship, that it was going to be short-lived," Allen said.

"What do you know about Peter's relationship with Cheryl or Florence?" Kadelack asked.

"Peter and I had been traveling together for about six months trying to find a position before landing one here. He's from California, and I'm from Iowa. We met in dramatics class at Berkley," Roselyn replied.

"Was the relationship___?" Kadelack began to ask.

He never had the chance to finish the question before she interrupted, "No, although he thought it would be. It was strictly about the theatre."

"Did he have a relationship with Florence that you know of?"

"Not that I know of personally, but he embarrassed her one day at the theatre during rehearsal. It was obvious that if they had a relationship, it was only to get the part in the play. Peter's like that. There's no obstacle to what he wants. I call it the spoiled California syndrome," Roselyn said.

"Do either of you know whether Cheryl or Florence own a hand gun?"

After looking at each other to confirm they didn't, Allen replied, "No."

Kadelack, looking back at Ben asked, "Is there anything you want to ask?

"No John, you pretty well covered it."

"Then we can go?" Allen asked.

"That's about all we wanted to ask. Thanks for coming in," Kadelack said.

After they left the office, Ben frustratingly said, "It looks like we have several people that were capable of wanting him dead. If Cheryl was so domineering, and he was about to break off the relationship, that's a motive. Sam, wanting revenge for his daughter being beaten, might have suspected Carl, and that's a motive. Florence thinking she was going to be his protector and was shunned by her advances. It's an outside chance, but that's also a motive. It seems like we're right back where we started."

Kadelack thought for a moment then opened his desk drawer. Taking out the plastic evidence bag with the broken piece of watch band, he examined it and said, "Do you remember the watch we saw on Florence's end table?"

A glimmer of hope crossed Davis' face, "Yes I do. She said it was Peter's, and mentioned she was taking it to the jewelry shop on Main Street to be repaired."

"That's right. Why don't we take it there and see if it matches the break?"

Arriving at Main Street, they entered the shop. An older man was behind the counter wearing an eye loop, examining a piece of jewelry. He looked up.

"Can I help you gentleman?" he asked.

"I don't know. Maybe you can."

Seemingly confused at his statement, he replied, "If it's about getting change for the parking meter out front, no, I don't have change.

I get that request a 100 times a day. Don't get caught with it expired though. The damn police around here are quick to write a ticket."

Approximating a smile at each other, Kadelack took out his badge, identifying himself and Davis.

Kadelack realizing he was trying to recover from his admonishment of the police for writing tickets, said,

"No, I understand your frustration."

Taking out the piece of watch band, he laid it on the glass counter.

"I wanted to ask you if a watch was brought in today with a broken band?"

Looking over the piece the jeweler replied, "Not so far today," pulling down his eye loop to examine it a little closer.

"That's a piece of band from a Rolex, isn't it?" the jeweler asked.

"That's what I was going to ask you," Kadelack replied. "How can you tell?"

Taking off the eye loop as though the question was insulting, he replied, "30 years in the business. That's how I can tell."

"I didn't mean to challenge your expertise. I was just asking as a matter of fact. I'm sorry you took it the wrong way."

"No harm done. Now how can I help you?"

"Is there any other jewelry shops on Main Street that repairs watch bands?"

"Repair: No. but I don't think the other shops cater to watches as much as just selling jewelry. I've been here for years. Most people that want a repair would come in here."

"This piece of watch-band is part of an investigation. If someone comes in with a watch with missing links like this, would you call me at this number?"

As Kadelack and Davis headed for the door, the shop-keeper said, "I can tell you who it belongs to already."

Returning to the counter Kadelack asked, "You can?"

"Yes, it belonged to a kid that came in a while ago. He said, 'He broke the band, when him and his girlfriend were moving furniture into their apartment.' Take this jeweler's loop. Do you see that small mark there just before the clasp? That's the mark I put on jewelry I repair. If someone brings something back that they say wasn't repaired right, all I have to do is look for that mark. It's made quite a few liars out of people wanting a free repair."

"Do you happen to remember the kid's name and what he looked like?" Kadelack asked.

"Just a minute; I keep a record of all my expensive watch repairs."

Taking out a ledger, he opened it. Running his index finger down the page, he stopped.

"Here it is. His name's Peter Austin. His address is 51 Holcombe Street, 2nd Floor. There's no phone number though."

He paused for a moment, but suddenly remembered.

"That's right. He said he didn't have one at the time because he was just moving into his new apartment. Like I said, he broke it moving furniture. I remember when he picked it up there was an attractive young girl with him. She seemed really excited they were moving in together. That's all I remember."

"Thanks a lot."

Kadelack left his card, and said, "If the watch shows up, would you call me?"

Adjusting his eye loop to continue examining jewelry, without looking up he replied, "Certainly."

Exiting the shop, Kadelack said, "It's after 4 o'clock. I wonder if Florence is going to bring it in at all."

"I don't know. Why don't we go by Peter's and see if he's there?" Davis asked.

Pulling up to 51 Holcombe Street, Kadelack looked at the names over the few door-bells.

"Here it is. P. Austin, 2nd floor."

Kadelack pushed the buzzer and a voice answered over the intercom.

"Who's there?"

"It's Detective's Kadelack and Davis. We'd like to have a few words with you."

"Wait a minute, I'll buzz you in." Peter replied.

Davis heard the buzzer, and opened the door. Getting to the apartment, the door was already open. The detective's stepping in, saw him packing cardboard boxes.

"Are you moving?" Davis asked.

"Yes. What did you officers want to ask me?"

"Do you own a Rolex wrist watch?" Davis asked.

Peter looked around as if he misplaced it.

"Yes, I haven't worn it for a few days. I think the band's getting loose again. Why?"

"Can we see it?" Davis asked.

"No problem. Just let me finish packing these few things away."

He paused briefly, holding a small teddy bear endearingly, as if he was remembering a fond moment. After gently placing it in a cardboard box, he closed the lid and ran a wide piece of tape over the folds.

"There, that's another box for the trip," Peter said.

"Where are you moving to?" Kadelack asked.

"I'm putting this stuff in storage- I think the play's about to finish. I'm getting kind of tired running all over the country trying to become a star. I give up."

"Well, can we see the watch?" Davis asked again.

Peter moved a few things off the end tables as if the watch might have been hidden from view. He suddenly stopped.

"I don't seem to see it here. Wait a minute. I'll check the bedroom."

Returning, he scratched his head, seemingly trying to remember.

"I can't seem to find it. I hope I didn't drop it when I was drunk the other night. I was pretty well lit."

"Were you out drinking alone?"

"No, I was with Florence, Charles and Carl at a bar."

"Which bar? Do you remember?"

"Yes, the Lambertville Tavern. Charles was talking about closing the play. Like I said, I think it's about done anyway. With Jan dead, I see no reason to stay in this part of the country. I'm heading back to California where the winters are warmer."

"Do you distinctly remember wearing the watch that evening?"

Pausing trying to remember, he said, "Wait. Now I remember. I remember noticing it was loose when I was sitting at the bar. I took it off and put it in my pocket. I must have lost it. That's a damn shame."

"Yeah, I'd be pissed too if I lost something that expensive," Davis said.

"It's not so much the expense, which I'm sure it was, but my father gave me that watch after graduating from college."

"We saw a watch with a broken band on an end table at Florence's, could that have been it?" Davis asked.

"I guess it could have been. Like I said, I was pretty well lit that night. She took me to her place to sleep it off, but of course, you know that already. I was there when you came in."

"Well, if it turns up, give us a call. Oh, by the way. Until this investigation is over, I don't want you leaving town," Davis said.

"I won't, but I'm not going to be living here after this week. I'm supposed to be moving back to Ethel's Boarding House. If you want me, that's where I'll be."

After leaving the apartment, Davis mentioned to Kadelack, "Did you notice how he was holding that teddy bear before packing it away? I wonder if it was Jan's."

"Yes, I did notice. Another thing, he's not moving in with Cheryl or Florence either. We suspected he had a relationship with Florence after seeing him there that morning. We just assumed he did. I think it's time to confront Florence with why she was driving Sam's car to the car wash, and looking around the area where we found the towel."

"We assume she was looking for something," Kadelack said. "Suppose she had put the broken piece of the watch band where she thought it might be found along with the towel. When she couldn't find it, maybe she thought it was found."

"That's a good possibility. If it is, she's trying to set Peter up getting him involved in this thing."

"That's the only reason I can think of. I wonder if this is her revenge for Peter using her as a stepping stone to stardom."

Chapter 15

Arriving at Florence's apartment complex, Kadelack and Davis saw Florence entering the building. Knowing it was the perfect opportunity to confront her, they hurried into the lobby. She was standing at the elevator when they walked in. Turning, pretending to just notice them, she said trying to mask her nervousness, "What! more questions?"

"I'm afraid so. Can we come to your apartment for this interview?" Kadelack asked.

"Sure, why not," she replied.

After Florence opened the door, they went inside.

"Have a seat. Would you like some coffee, or perhaps a drink?" she asked.

"No, I don't think so," they replied.

"Well, this has been a hectic day. I sure need one," she said.

While she was in the kitchen making her drink, Ben tapped Kadelack on the arm, pointing to the wrist watch still on the end table. He said loud enough for Florence to hear, "Peter's going to be pissed at you isn't he?"

A few seconds of silence before Florence returned to the living room.

"Why would he be pissed at me?" she asked in a lower tone.

Davis pointing to the watch said, "You never took his watch to get repaired."

Shrugging it off as if it was unimportant, she replied, "I guess you're right. I was so busy, I forgot all about it. I'll have to do it tomorrow. Now what did you want to ask me?"

"Do you have a relationship with Sam outside the theatre?" Kadelack asked.

Pausing for a moment from stirring the ice cubes in her drink, she looked up, becoming defensive.

"We had a couple encounters- What the hell does that have to do with

Carl's death?"

"I didn't ask that question to want to know your personal business. Detective Davis and I saw you at the car wash the morning Carl was found. That's why I asked."

It was obvious he struck a nerve. Her face turned red and took on the look of skepticism, putting her drink down on the coffee table. "Why is that important to this investigation? I told you, we used to date years ago when he was involved in the financial end of the theatre. In fact, if it wasn't for his money, the theatre wouldn't have been built."

"I thought it was Charles Cohen's money behind the productions," Davis asked.

"Yes, the productions. But Sam was the one who purchased the property and paid for the conversions to a theatre. The old mill was in pretty bad shape. His wife had recently died, and I guess overseeing the project was just what he needed. That's when we began seeing each other."

"What did you do after you left the car wash?" Kadelack asked.

Realizing he saw her there and may have followed, she didn't answer immediately, giving it some thought. She realized she was trapped, and had no choice but to bluff her way, hoping she wasn't followed. Like a poker player, she tried not to give away the weakness of the cards she held, but finally realized she had no alternative.

"I took a ride along the river. I was bringing Sam's car back to him."

"We know. We followed you to Sam's, and continued to follow you until he dropped you off at the theatre," Kadelack said.

Looking down at the floor, she said, "Then I don't think I have to answer that. You already know."

Kadelack slapped the palms of his hands on both knees as he stood up.

"I think that's about it. Why don't you come with us to police headquarters? You can tell us everything you know about what happened to Carl."

Florence put on her coat. "Look, I didn't have anything to do with him being murdered, but I'll tell you what I do know," she replied defensively.

"Well, whether you do or don't, I don't want you to say anymore until we get to my office. I have to read you the Miranda Rights, just in case there are charges to be brought against you," Kadelack said.

She chose to remain silent until they arrived at the office. After taking off her coat, Kadelack offered her a chair next to his desk. Detective Davis, not wanting to confuse the questioning, sat on the edge of another desk to listen.

Kadelack began by reading her rights and asked if she wanted a lawyer present.

"No, detective, I don't need the lawyer, but I know who will," she said.

Taken by surprise, they looked at her. Kadelack asked, "You mean to tell me you definitely know who killed Carl?"

"Yes."

"Were you there when it happened?"

"Yes, but as I said, I didn't have anything to do with it."

"Before we begin, do you mind if I put on this tape recorder? It makes my job a little easier."

"No, I don't mind."

"Okay, start from the beginning. What happened?" Kadelack asked.

"It actually started when Jan was murdered. Sam initially thought Charles was the one that beat up Jan. He knew she had seen him a few times intimately."

"Did he say how he knew that?"

"Yes, He came to my apartment one evening to ask me whether I ever saw them together- you know, kissing or close personal contact. I told him, 'No, why would she bother with someone over twice her age?' That's when he told me he was having Charles followed. He told me the private detective he hired followed them to Charles' office one night, and they stayed for several hours. I think that's when he must have confronted Charles in his driveway. That was after Jan was beaten on New Year's Eve."

"Do you know if Charles was the one that did it?

"No, I always suspected Carl. I know personally he can be abusive. But I don't want to get into that unless it's necessary."

"I already suspected you had an intimate relationship, but as you said, I won't get into that," Kadelack said.

"How do you know that?" Florence asked.

"Well, Carl was so concerned you might have thought he had something to do with Jan's death. He told Allen and Roselyn."

"At the time I did."

"What made you suspect that?" Kadelack asked.

"Well, I guess it's necessary to get into my personal experiences with Carl. There's no other way to tell you without doing it. It started out with him asking for more instructions on how to act: positioning, hand gestures, the little things that bring a character to life."

"Was this before or after he got the part?"

"It was within a few days after the play started. I mentioned to him that he had to put more feeling into the person he's playing. He seemed to be really into his part, and I thought it was purely acting. Once in awhile, he would touch me where it wasn't necessary as I was instructing him. I let it go a few times before I finally had to mention it. He stopped, but I remember the look on his face. He seemed very annoyed at me for mentioning it."

"When did you start the relationship?"

She looked at Kadelack, and he could tell she was sorry for ever mentioning it to anyone for obvious reasons.

"I remember when I was coming down from the office one night- Allen and Carl were coming from the men's dressing room. I overheard Allen say very forcefully to him, 'Roselyn would appreciate if you don't make advances at her. Her and I are an item.' That was right after I corrected him."

"What did he say to Allen?"

"He apologized as they walked down the hall toward the exit. I did hear Allen say, 'I think Roselyn would like to hear the apology from you personally.'"

"And did you ever find out whether he did?" Kadelack asked.

"Yes, I told Roselyn I overheard the conversation, and asked her what it was about. She told me about the incident, and I asked if she wanted me to speak to him since I was in charge of the production."

"What did she say?"

"That's when she told me Allen straightened it out. Since she never had the problem again, I assumed it was a one-time incident. Detective, do you mind if I have a drink of water?"

"No, I'm sorry for not asking. I was so intent listening to your story,"

Kadelack said.

"And that's not an understatement," Davis added.

Kadelack temporarily turned off the recorder, got up and brought back a glass of water. Turning on the recorder again, he continued.

"If you knew Roselyn had a problem with him, what made you get involved?"

"That's a good question, now that it's over. At the time we had a few conversations about his personal life, and I began to feel sorry for him. He said he recently moved to the area and didn't have any friends. It started with him taking me out to dinner, then us going back to my apartment, listening to some music over a drink. In spite of his faults, he was very interesting, extremely intelligent," pausing briefly, "Perhaps feeling sorry for what happened to him."

"You were going to tell me when he became abusive," Kadelack said.

Snapping back to reality, she continued, "At first he was very gentle with sex, but it seemed the more familiar we became, the more abusive he was. I mentioned it several times and he would lay off the rough stuff for awhile, then after a few times, would gradually go back to it. Once he grabbed me by the neck and squeezed as he was climaxing. I thought he was going to strangle me, so I punched at his face. It seemed to bring him back to reality. I was glad it worked."

"Do you think that's what might have happened to Jan on New Year's Eve?"

"I'm not positive, and it's only my opinion, but yes."

"What, if anything, do you know about his relationship with Cheryl?"

"I don't know that much about their sexual relationship. I do know Cheryl can be domineering," she said.

"Is that a personal observation?" Kadelack asked.

"Yes, and she made no bones about displaying it in anyone else's company. In fact, Carl came from the dressing room just before the play began several days before he was murdered. He had a bandage wrapped around his right forearm. When I asked him what happened, he frustratingly replied, 'What do you think?' I took it that Cheryl had something to do with it."

The detectives looked at each other, remembering what the medical examiner said about the stab wound not being an accident.

"Let's get down to what you witnessed when Carl was killed," Kadelack continued.

Turning away, she was reluctant to start for a moment.

"Well, what do you have to tell me about that?" Kadelack asked.

Facing him again she replied, "As I said, Sam always wanted revenge for Jan's beating. He came to me about a week ago and asked if I would help him square a debt. I asked him what the debt was. That's when he told me what he intended to do. I knew he can be hot-tempered, so I asked him why he just didn't pay someone to do it."

Kadelack interrupted, "So it was Sam that did it?"

"No, Sam only wanted the satisfaction of beating him. That must be the Irish in him. He certainly has enough money and knows enough people to let someone else do it."

"Was Sam's car used the night Carl was murdered?"

"Yes, that's why..."

Stopping short, she realized she could be charged with being an accessory to a crime by destroying evidence. Kadelack looked her in the eye.

"Was Carl killed in Sam's car?" he asked.

"No, his body was only transported in it."

"Tell me what happened the night he was murdered."

"I have to tell you what her character's like, so you'll fully appreciate what happened, Florence said.

"You said her. Who is her?" Kadelack asked.

"Cheryl. I don't know whether you were aware of it, but Carl was going to leave her. As I said before, she can be very vindictive holding a grudge against a person, but I never knew the extreme she would go to get back at someone. She took things personally that she had no way of controlling. I told her, we don't always have control of what someone does. She began a relationship with Peter while he was still unsure of getting his part in the play. I think he was also playing me to secure his part since we went out a few times, but I didn't find that out until later."

Looking down at the floor, she seemed more remorseful than a person who witnessed a crime.

"What does that have to do with Carl?" kadelack asked.

She took a deep breath then exhaled. Looking toward the window, she was reluctant to answer, but finally confessed, "It doesn't. But I want to clear my conscience of everything that went on, including Jan's death."

Surprised at the statement, Kadelack sat back then looked at Davis.

"So you believe she killed Jan too?" Kadelack asked.

"I know she did."

"Tell me about it."

"Jan and Peter were seeing each other and decided to get an apartment together."

"Was this after he had the relationship with Cheryl?"

"Yes. I think Cheryl took the relationship with Peter too seriously. Like I said, he played me the same way. After several weeks of living with her, he began seeing her domineering ways. Shortly after he reunited with Jan, they decided to get an apartment together."

"Is that why she killed Jan?"

"Probably. Like I said, she hates losing, especially with her love life. I went to the theatre the day Jan was murdered. As I was approaching the costume room, I was shocked to see Cheryl trying to carry Jan's body in. It was too heavy for her, so she put her down and drug her by the arms the rest of the way."

"Was Jan already dead?" Kadelack asked.

"I thought she was."

"Didn't you say anything to Cheryl?"

"Yes, I screamed at her, 'What the hell's going on?'"

"Didn't she try to hide the fact you saw what was happening?"

"No, she was getting ready to answer me when Jan began to move."

Florence paused for a moment and looked at detective Davis before continuing. "She went to the prop room closet and began moving things around on a shelf, like she was looking for something. A few things fell out on the floor, and one of the things was a ship's bell with a white knotted rope attached. She took the rope off, bent down and wrapped it around Jan's neck and began to twist it. I tried to get her to stop, but she was just crazed, pushing me away. After I fell backwards, she began twisting the rope again until Jan stopped breathing."

"You mean she just cold bloodedly finished what she set out to do?"

"Yes."

"Didn't you ask her why she did it?"

"I believe she already realized I knew why she did it. It was because Peter was leaving her for Jan."

"You mean she mentioned it?"

"No, but I know that's what it was about."

"Did you mention any of this to Charles or Sam? Why didn't you go to the police?"

"I was afraid I would be implicated, and I knew Sam would never forgive me for helping Cheryl."

"Is that the only reason?"

"No, we had a sexual relationship, she threatened to expose."

"Expose it to who- Charles?"

"No, Charles wouldn't have cared, but I knew Sam's distain for anyone that practices that kind of lifestyle. I think that's one of the reasons he left being involved with the theatre."

"How long did you have a relationship with Cheryl?"

"Too long: That's why I know personally she can be domineering. In fact, she used it to her advantage."

"What was that advantage?"

"She became more aggressive with her input in the theatre productions, that's why she had a part in almost every play."

"So did you help her hide Jan's body behind the clothing rack?"

"Yes. When we heard Edward come into the theatre...."

"Edward- Edward the gardener?"

"Yes."

"He's the one whose wife was sick. We interviewed him first. Then again after that," Kadelack said.

"That's right. He was in a rush to get home, and left still wearing his stage clothes. He knew Jan was picky about the wardrobe room, so he wanted to return them," Florence said.

"What did you do then?" Kadelack asked.

"I closed the door, and we hid behind the clothing rack. He knocked, then opened the door calling Jan's name. After he closed the door and walked away, I figured he was going up to the office, so I opened the door and looked. When he was up there, Cheryl and I headed for the fire exit door in the rear of the seating area. It's pretty dark in that section when the lights are off. We heard him call out again, but we didn't answer and just stayed crouched behind the seats. When we thought he wasn't looking, we pushed the door open and made our exit."

"Let me take your statement back to when you saw Cheryl drag Jan's body. Is that what caused the black marks on the floor?" Kadelack asked.

"Yes, I saw them, but we didn't have time to erase them. I went back later and did it."

"Was that before the cleaning crew came in?"

"Yes, Jan was already dead, so it really didn't matter."

"Tell me what happened to Carl."

"Cheryl called me that night and told me Carl was going to leave her. She asked if I could help convince him to reconsider. When I asked if she wanted me to meet with him privately, she suggested we should all go to the Lambertville Tavern for a drink to celebrate the closing of the show. It would probably be the last time we would be together."

"Did you discuss it with anyone else?"

"I mentioned it to Roselyn and Allen, but they weren't interested, so it was just going to be the four of us, Cheryl, Carl, Peter and myself."

Before she continued, Kadelack asked, "Was Charles invited?"

Florence looked at him, surprised that he knew Charles was there.

"No, Charles must have had other plans," she said.

Becoming aggressive, Kadelack said, "We know for a fact, he was not only there, but sort of had to baby sit Peter that was, as he said, 'Plastered.'"

Trying not to make eye contact again, she recanted, "Yes, he was there- but not with us. Charles didn't know we were going there. He was supposed to meet a girl that never showed."

"How did you know that?"

She realized she was caught in another lie.

"Charles saw us come in, but didn't join us. The only reason he wouldn't have, would be because he was meeting someone else. He called me about

1:30 to come and pick Peter up, and I had to go back."

"Was Carl already dead at this point?"

"Yes."

"Tell me about it."

"When we were at the table, Cheryl went to the bathroom. She did it on purpose to give me a chance to ask Carl whether he was going to leave her. When I asked, he looked at me and said, 'No way, you know what she can be like. I'm definitely leaving. I heard you know about that personally too.' I remember looking at him, realizing Cheryl must have told him about our relationship. When Cheryl returned, she looked at me for an answer, and I shook my head motioning that he refused."

"Is that when she decided to kill him?"

"I didn't think so at the time, but when they were getting ready to leave, Cheryl suggested we go to my apartment and continue to celebrate. I didn't think there was anything I could do or say to change his mind, but I think Cheryl wanted me to try once more."

Kadelack tried to trip her up in another lie.

"Did Peter go with you?" he asked.

"No, he was sitting at the table with his head resting on his folded arms. He was too drunk to go, so we just left him in Charles' charge."

She passed Kadelack's little test. He already knew from Charles that Peter was there until he called Florence to pick him up around 1:45.

"So you left with Carl and Cheryl? Was Carl killed in your apartment?"

"Yes."

"What happened there?"

"Shortly after we walked in, I went to the kitchen to mix a few drinks. That's when I heard Cheryl pleading with him not to leave her. There were a few heated words, but I don't remember what they were. I didn't want to interfere so I stayed in the kitchen until I thought they were finished. As I was coming from the kitchen, I saw Carl putting on his coat. As his back was turned, Cheryl pulled a small gun from her pocket, put it to the back of his head and pulled the trigger."

"What did Cheryl do then?"

"She acted like she was stunned by her own actions. I really think she did it out of a heated passion. She just seemed to stand over him slumped over on the sofa for a few minutes not doing anything. When I saw the blood begin coming from the bullet wound, I quickly went to the bathroom and got a towel to wrap around his head."

"Was that towel discarded at the place where you dumped Carl's body?"

"Yes."

"Carl was too big for both of you to carry. Who helped you get rid of it?"

"We stood there staring at Carl's lifeless body for a few moments, trying to decide what to do. That's when I decided to call Sam."

"Did you tell him what happened?"

"No, I just told him I desperately needed his help with something."

"What time was that?"

"It was about 12:30. I remember him asking me, 'Can't it wait until morning?' I told him no. It was something that couldn't wait. I think that's what made him want to get here in a hurry. He was here in about 15 minutes."

"What did he say when he got there?"

"The first thing he noticed after coming in the door was Carl. He asked, 'What the hell happened?' I told him Cheryl shot him."

"Was Cheryl in the room, when Sam came in?"

"No, she was in the bathroom."

"What did he say about Carl?" Kadelack asked.

"Actually, nothing. I think he was glad Carl was dead. I think he even mentioned something about being poetic justice, but I don't remember his exact words."

"How did you get the body out without being seen?"

"Sam drove his car around to the fire exit in the rear of the building. He came back upstairs, and the three of us carried him down and put him in the back seat. We drove him about a mile south on 32, and Sam pulled over where he thought we wouldn't be seen. We carried him over the small foot bridge and dumped him in the canal. On the way back to the car, Cheryl suddenly stopped and said, 'I think we left the towel on the bank of the canal. I'll go back and get it.' When she returned, Sam told her, 'Throw the damn thing away.' and took it from her, tossing it in the high grass."

"What did you do then?"

"Sam's house is closer to where we dumped the body, so he told me to drop him off first. Then take his car home."

"Is that why you took it to the car wash?"

"Yes, I didn't want Sam to be more involved than he already was."

"Right near where we found the towel, we found a piece of a Rolex watch band. Was it part of the crime?"

Florence appeared to be confused by the question. "Not as far as I know, why?" she asked.

"When we followed you from the car wash, you stopped at the spot where we had already removed the towel. You were looking around for something, what was it?"

Looking confused, she glanced at Davis, then back at Kadelack, but didn't answer.

Kadelack continued in a stern voice, "I'll tell you what you were looking for. You were looking to see if the piece of broken watch-ban was discovered when we found the towel. We did find it! We took it to a jewelry shop on Main Street and the owner identified it as a part he repaired on Peter's watch. We saw the broken watch on the end table in your apartment. Now why did you plant it there?"

Florence realized the detectives knew Peter was incapacitated and still at the bar when the murder happened, and didn't have an immediate answer.

After some thought, she said, "I think Cheryl might have dropped it there. When I picked the watch up the next morning to take it to the jeweler, the broken piece was missing."

"Was Cheryl at your apartment that morning?"

"No, I mean yes. Well, I mean she stopped by. After she left, that's when I was going to take the watch to the jeweler's. He's only a few blocks away from the car wash. She must have taken it before we carried Carl out."

The story wasn't adding up. She was lying and they knew it. Continuing to give her enough rope, they knew she would eventually hang herself if it wasn't corroborated with Cheryl or Sam.

"I have a question?" Kadelack continued.

"What's that?" she replied.

"Sam didn't just help get rid of Carl's body by thinking he got what he deserves. What was it?"

She hesitated,

"I knew something about Sam's business affairs he'd rather not be known."

"What was it?" Kadelack asked.

"His business wouldn't have survived without help."

"What are you referring to- financial help from someone? Someone in the banking business?" Davis asked.

Florence looked at him, then back at Kadelack. "Yes, the mob in South Philly, and I think from New York, but I'm not sure," she said.

"What was he supposed to do for the cash?"

"He was helping to do something through his business."

"What kind of business is he in?"

"Sam and Charles were in the shipping business together. When they split partnerships, Sam was short of money to buy Charles out completely, so he borrowed."

Taking a chance on getting her to say what that business may have been, Kadelack asked,

"Did it have something to do with the drug trade?"

Florence looked back at him.

"I don't think Sam would have done that. It was probably something else. Like I said, I don't really know."

"Getting back to what happened after you dropped Sam off at his home, what did you do then?"

"I dropped Cheryl off at her apartment; then went home."

"You picked Peter up at the bar. How did you know he was there?"

"I wasn't home very long before the phone rang. It was Charles asking me to pick up Peter. I was surprised when Charles told me he was still at the bar. He said he was trying to make Peter come out of his hangover by feeding him black coffee the bartender made."

"What time was that?"

"About 20 minutes to 2:00. When I got there, he was pretty much coming out of it. I was pissed at him because it was something I really didn't need after what I went through, and the heavy downpour wasn't making it any more pleasant."

Kadelack looked at Ben, then back at Florence.

"We already know that. Charles told us you acted disgusted having to deal with him. Then what did you do?" Kadelack asked.

"I drove him to his apartment, but he couldn't find his key, so I took him to my apartment."

"When you picked him up, did you use Sam's car?"

"No, I used my own. After we got in, I put him to bed, took a shower and went to bed myself. When I woke up in the morning, I woke him and told him to take a shower. That's when you came to the apartment."

The room fell silent for a few moments before Kadelack turned off the recorder. Florence looked at him as though he was going to ask another question off the record. Instead, he sent a statement that was like a shock wave. Something she thought she could possibly avoid.

"Florence, I hope you realize by your confession, it's up to the district attorney if there's going to be a prosecution against you with these crimes."

"I realize that. I just want to get it all out in the open."

"Well, we appreciate your statement. It clears up quite a few loose ends. I have to tell you, this thing is far from over. You'll have to stay close to New Hope in case we want another interview."

Sighing as though a great load had been lifted from her shoulders, she stood up. Ben picked up her coat, and helped her put it on. Before leaving the room, she looked over her shoulder.

"Thanks, Detective Davis," she said.

She turned to Kadelack. "Whenever you need me, call."

After Florence closed the door, Davis turned to Kadelack, shaking his head in disbelief.

"John, did you notice something in her interview? Half of her confession was like she was acting. I'm beginning to think we can't believe any of these people. They act as if it's a stage play."

"Yes, I know. I was thinking the same thing. I'm wondering whether we should arrest Cheryl on Florence's statement, or just bring her in for an interview? As you said, it's like a stage play. So far, we have Florence's word against whatever Cheryl might say."

"Maybe we should bring in Sam first," Davis said. "Let's find out if he can shed some more light on Florence's story. If he's hesitant to talk to us, we could always confront him with the fact he could be prosecuted for helping get rid of Carl's body."

"That's a better idea. I'll call him now," Kadelack said.

After Kadelack dialed Sam's number, the phone was picked up by the third ring.

"Hello, who's calling?"

"This is Detective Kadelack, New Hope Police Department. Is Sam Doherty there?"

"This is his wife, officer, just a moment. I'll get him. He's in his office."

He could hear her tell Sam it was the police department, and he could hear Sam's reply, "What does he want?"

"I don't know. I guess you'll find out. Here's the phone."

"Hello, this is Sam Doherty. How can I help you?"

"Sam, this is Detective Kadelack. I'd like you to come to my office today."

He hesitated to answer until Kadelack said, "It's about Carl Dunn's death."

"When do you want me to come in?" Sam quickly replied.

"Now, if it's possible."

Realizing the urgency of his request, Sam looked at his watch.

"I'll be there in about 20 minutes."

"Fine, I'll see you then."

Chapter 16

"Officer Kadelack, what's this about?" Sam said as he entered the room.

"Mr. Dougherty-," Kadelack said.

"Please," he replied. "Just call me Sam."

"Okay, Sam. We had Florence in here this afternoon, and she told us the whole story about how Carl was killed, and that you helped her and Cheryl get rid of his body."

Looking surprised, he became defensive.

"Am I being charged with anything?" Sam asked.

"Not yet. Not unless the district attorney says so. But there are some pretty serious charges here," Kadelack said.

"I had no alternative. I was taken completely by surprise. I had no idea she was going to do it."

Kadelack and Davis quickly glanced at each other.

"Wait a minute, are you trying to tell us you were there?" Kadelack asked.

Looking confused, Sam replied, "Yes, isn't that the reason I'm here?"

"In a way yes, but let us hear your version of what happened."

"Florence called me about 12:30 that night and said Carl wanted to talk to me about Jan's death. He wanted to tell me what really happened. I was about to get in bed, but I was so interested in what he had to say, I agreed to go to Florence's apartment, pick her up, then drive to Cheryl's and pick up her and Carl. When I pulled into the parking lot at Cheryl's, Carl was standing in the doorway alone."

"You mean Cheryl wasn't there?"

"No, I asked Florence if we were supposed to wait for her, but she didn't answer. She got out of the car and spoke to Carl for a few moments, then got back in the car. Carl was in the front seat, and she took a back seat behind him. I asked again if we were supposed to wait for Cheryl, and Carl said, 'No, I'd rather not get her involved.' Then we drove away."

"Did you go to Florence's apartment?"

"We were heading in that direction. I was listening to Florence and Carl in a discussion about Cheryl."

"Do you remember what the discussion was about?"

"It had something to do with Carl supposedly leaving Cheryl. All of a sudden Carl said, 'Sam, can you pull over for a minute? There's something I want to get straight.' I pulled into the parking lot of Florence's apartment complex, and he turned to face me. I expected him to tell me about the relationship he had with Jan. Instead, he told me there was no relationship with Jan. Somehow, he found out it was Charles that had a relationship with her all along. I think Peter coming into the picture was becoming a problem."

"What did he tell you about Charles's relationship with Jan?"

"He told me he saw Jan get into Charles's car on New Year's Eve after leaving the Lambertville Tavern. I told him the private detective's report said he didn't see her leave with him."

"Well, if he told you that, then who did she leave with?" Kadelack asked.

"He swore up and down she left with Charles. He even suggested the private detective was paid off by Charles to change the report."

"And you believed him?"

"The sincerity in his voice almost made it believable. I never trusted Charles to begin with, and maybe my opinion was prejudiced. I wouldn't put it past him."

"What was Florence doing while this conversation was taking place?"

"She was sitting in the back seat listening to what he had to say. She did interfere once when he blamed Charles. I think they may have had a relationship together off and on. Florence is a free spirit, if you know what I mean."

"Florence told us you and her had a relationship when you were financing the renovations of the theatre. Is that correct?"

Sam looked down at the floor. "Yes, and I think every actor that passes through the theatre has an affair with her."

"Were you aware of her making a gesture to Carl that he may have been the one that killed Jan?"

With a surprised look he replied, "No, I wasn't aware of that."

"According to Roselyn and Allen Simpson, Carl had a meeting with them voicing his concern about Florence insinuating he was the one that did it. Do you feel Florence's suspicions were only to mask her own guilt?"

"I don't know. I wouldn't have believed it if she didn't kill him and you asked that question," Sam replied.

"Was Carl killed in Florence's apartment?"

"No, he was killed in my car."

"How was she able to do it?"

"I never really knew what her intention was, but it's obvious now. She planned to kill him all along. After saying what he wanted to say about Jan's beating, he asked me for a cigarette," Sam continued. "When he leaned forward to light it, I saw her hand come forward with a small pistol. Before I could react, she put it to the back of his head and pulled the trigger. He slumped forward, and in shock, I said, 'What the fuck did you do that for?' She said, 'I know he's a liar. I believe he did kill Jan.'"

"What did you do then?" Kadelack asked.

"I told her to go get a towel from her apartment. When she came back she wrapped the towel around his head, and we drove south on 32. When we came to a secluded spot, I took him out, and she helped carry him over the small foot bridge, where we dumped him in the canal. After we were heading back to the car, she suddenly stopped. When I asked what was wrong, she said, 'I forgot to take the towel.' I asked, 'What the hell do you want that for?' but she didn't listen. When she came back, I grabbed it from her and threw it in the high grass. For some reason she was going to get it again, but after picking it up, she must have thought I was right, and put it back down."

"Then what did you do?"

"Since I live close by, I told her to drop me off and take my car home, then get it washed in the morning. She did, and that's all I know about it."

He seemed to be the only one of the group connected to the theatre that didn't have his words or actions choreographed.

"Do you know why she went back to the scene the next morning?" Kadelack asked.

"I didn't know she did. What was she doing?"

"That's what I would like you to tell me."

Pausing for a moment, trying to understand why she would, Sam said, "I haven't the slightest idea. Did she say?"

"No, but we found a piece of a watch band near where we picked up the blood-soaked towel. We traced it to a jeweler on Main Street. It was part of a watch band Peter had repaired some time ago. Do you think Florence would have left it on purpose, and if so, why?" Kadelack asked.

"I don't know. Maybe it has something to do with revenge against him. I know Florence came to me shortly after the play began and complained about Peter giving her a hard time with taking instructions."

"Do you mean she wanted your help to remove him from the play?"

"Yes, Jan brought Peter to the house one day to introduce him to me. I think she knew they would eventually be engaged and probably get married at some point in the near future. She told me about the friction between Florence and Peter and wanted me to somehow intercede for him."

"Did you?"

"I had no real influence with Charles, so I called Florence and asked her to go to dinner with me one evening. That's when I asked her to reconsider. At the time she agreed, but somehow the way she said it, looked as though they were just empty words. When I saw Jan later that evening, I asked her, 'Why don't you just let me give Peter a job with my company, and forget about being an actor?' She said, 'I'd rather let him try making his own way without help from anyone. If he wanted a job, his father has a pretty successful company on the West Coast.' I wasn't sure at the time whether she was telling the truth. For some unknown reason, we became a little distant after I remarried."

"Getting back on the subject as to why she was at the scene," Kadelack continued. "Is it your opinion Florence might have had more of a reason to plant a piece of evidence, hoping to get Peter involved in Carl's murder?"

"Knowing Florence, that may very well be. Have you had Cheryl in yet?"

"No, we want to clear things up with where Carl's attachment with

Florence might have been. When she gave her statement, she said Carl was in Cheryl's apartment when Cheryl shot him. She told us she called you after Cheryl did it, and asked you to help get rid of the body. We didn't quite believe her story. If she did shoot him there, chances are someone would have heard the shot. According to your story, he was killed in your car. Would you mind if we search it to see if there's any evidence?"

"No, I don't mind. I'm telling you the truth, but go right ahead. In fact, if someone will take me home, I can leave it here for you to do whatever you have to do." After handing Kadelack his car keys, he said, "I have another car at home. Is that all the questions you wanted to ask?"

"Yes, unless Cheryl says something you might be able to clear up. Come with me, I'll see to it one of the policeman gives you a ride home."

When Kadelack returned to the office, Davis asked, "Do you want me to call the lab and have someone come out to check the car?"

"Yes, there might be something that was missed when Florence got it cleaned. In the meantime I'm going to call Cheryl in. Let's hear what she has to say."

After dialing Cheryl's number, Kadelack asked her to come to his office for another interview. Her response was a little testy, but she agreed.

"I'll be there in about a half hour."

***

Walking in the door of Kadelack's office, Cheryl asked, "Is Sam here?"

Davis looked up. "What makes you ask that question?"

"That looks like Sam Dougherty's car on the lot. I was wondering if he's involved in some way with Carl's murder. It looks like two people are going over it?" Cheryl said.

"It does belong to Sam. He told us Florence was the one that shot Carl, and she did it in his car. When Florence was here giving her interview earlier, she told us you did it in her apartment."

Stunned at the remark, she said, "That bitch! She's a goddamn liar."

"Well what was your role in this thing?" Kadelack asked.

"I knew Carl was about to leave me, and asked Florence if she could possibly persuade him to change his mind."

"Was this the night you were at the bar celebrating with Florence, Carl and Peter?"

"Yes, I asked her earlier as we were leaving the theatre. While we were at our table, Peter noticed Charles sitting at the bar talking to the bartender. When he went to speak with him, I conveniently excused myself to go to the ladies room, giving her the opportunity to speak to Carl on my behalf."

"Did she?" Kadelack asked.

"When I got back to the table, Peter had returned, and was in a conversation with Carl. Peter's not a drinker and was already at his maximum capacity with alcohol, using Carl's shoulder to lean on, talked about Jan and their relationship. While they were distracted, I made a motion to Florence if she had a response, to what Carl's answer might have been. She took me aside and told me she hadn't had the opportunity since Peter was there. That's when she told me she asked Carl if he could meet her later. I knew that's why Carl was going out again after we got home."

"Then you knew making the excuse he was going out for cigarettes wasn't the reason he left?"

"Yes, when he never returned that night, I knew something was definitely wrong. You said Sam's car was involved. That means he was there. Is he the one that did it?"

"He said no during his interview. He said Florence did it. Do you know why?"

"I can only imagine it had something to do with Jan's death," Cheryl said.

"Why would she kill him over that? She said you were the one that did it."

Cheryl sat back in the chair in disbelief, saying, "She's a mental case. I had nothing to do with that. It was her."

Intently listening to Cheryl's statement, Kadelack bade her to continue.

"The day Jan was murdered I was coming to the theatre."

"Why?"

"Edward called my apartment and asked if I could open the theatre. He went home with his clothes he wears for the play and wanted to return them."

"Why didn't he keep them until the afternoon show?"

"It was Monday. We don't have a show Monday or Tuesday. He knows Jan's particular with the clothing everyone wears. In fact, she's particular about everything in the prop room. The prop room is like her private domain."

"What time was that?"

"It was about 9 a.m."

"When we interviewed Edward here at the theatre, he said you gave him the key at your apartment."

"I did. After he left, I remembered the key I gave him was the wrong key, so I went to the theatre. When I got there, the door was already unlocked so I thought someone already inside; left him in."

"Did you go in?"

"No, like I said, it's our days off, and I wanted to get my errands done early, so Carl and I could spend some time together. We were going to Baltimore to see the National Aquarium."

"Then you never entered the theatre at all?"

"No, it was exactly as I told you. I figured since the door was already unlocked, and Edward had the wrong key, Jan was already in there."

"What time did you get to the theatre after Jan was killed? When I started the investigation, it was about 2. Within the next 2 hours, most of the cast, including you and Carl were already there. You couldn't have possibly been in Baltimore," Kadelack said.

"Well, we never got started that day. By the time I ran my errands, it was too late to start out, so we decided to save it for another time."

"Then what were your movements that morning?"

Stopping to think of how she could document her movements, she looked at Kadelack, then at Davis.

"I guess you'll just have to take my word for it," she said in an unsteady voice.

The detectives looked at each other; then at Cheryl, trying to decide whether her statements were sincere. Her response to questions, were without hesitation, and with their years of experience questioning suspects, it was a positive sign she may be telling the truth. Unsure of Kadelack's next statement, she nervously waited. A deafening silence filled the room as she anticipated his reply.

After a few moments he asked, "Is there anyone that can account for your time between 10:00 and 11:00?"

Concentrating she replied, "I was so busy that day. Wait a minute. I can. When the police write a parking ticket, they put the time on it. I got one that day while I was having breakfast in the coffee shop. I was sitting at the counter at the front window when I noticed the cop writing it. I went out to plead with him that the meter must have just expired. I told him I was so busy I forgot. He recognized me from the theatre, and we had a 10-minute chat about my performance in the play. I thought he was going to let me slide without getting one, but he explained that once he started writing the ticket, there's no way he could cancel. He gave it to me anyway."

Retrieving the summons from her car, she handed it to Kadelack, "Here it is."

Kadelack looked at it to verify her claim.

As he was looking at it, she added, "The officer's name is at the bottom. I'm sure he'll remember talking to me."

"I'm going to keep this. Don't worry about paying it on time. If there's nothing else you can tell us, you can go."

Looking relieved she had documentation accounting for her time, she said, "How do I handle seeing Florence?"

"You won't have to worry about that."

"Why not?"

Not wanting to divulge their next move, Kadelack dismissed her question. After Davis helped her on with her jacket, he saw her to the door.

"Thanks for coming in. We'll let you know if we have any more questions you might be able to clear up," Davis said.

After closing the door, Davis turned to Kadelack and leaned against it.

"What do you think? Shall we get a warrant for Florence?" he asked.

"I'd like to get a warrant to search her apartment and her office at the theatre first. We may just find something to definitely tie her in with the murder. Let me check the chem. lab people going over Sam's car and see if they found anything."

Just as Kadelack was about to walk out the door, it opened, and a member of the team searching Sam's vehicle entered the room.

"Well, did you find anything?" Kadelack anxiously asked.

"We gave it a good going over. That car's as clean as can be. There isn't even a print on the passenger side or the rear seats. It's been wiped clean."

"Thanks for the effort," Kadelack said.

Turning to Davis, he said, "I guess we don't have any alternative but to search her apartment. I'll type out a warrant and call the district judge and ask if he'll sign it."

"Do you think we should include the theatre office in the warrant?"

"Yes, but I'd like to search the apartment first."

"Do you think Florence will be home so we can execute it?"

Taking a blank warrant from a wall cabinet, Kadelack looked over his shoulder, answering.

"We'll know that when we get there."

Within a few minutes it was completed, ready for the judge to sign.

Arriving at Florence's apartment complex, they knocked at her door. After opening it, she stepped back, surprised to see them.

"What? More questions?"

"Not this time, Florence. We're here to serve a search warrant for your apartment. Sign it at the bottom where you see the X," Kadelack said.

She tried covering her nervousness by asking, "What are you looking for?"

"It says it on the warrant. Read it. 'Unspecified.' That means any evidence found concerning this case."

"Maybe if you tell me what it is, I'll get it for you," Florence said.

"That's alright. But if you care to accompany us while we're looking, you can."

Starting the search in the living room where she said Carl was shot didn't reveal anything. Continuing to the bedroom, they searched the dresser drawers and closets. The more they searched, the more frustrated Florence became as she watched them go through her personal belongings.

Finally, realizing their search was in vain, Kadelack said, "Florence, the warrant is also for your office at the theatre. Would you like to accompany us?"

"I thought you came here to look over the crime scene," Florence snapped back. "I told you Cheryl did it. Are you looking for something she may have left behind?"

"Don't be upset. We haven't accused anyone yet," Davis said.

She seemed relieved, thinking they were still looking for evidence pertaining to Cheryl's part in the crime, and she mellowed.

"I think that's about it for here," Kadelack said to Davis, "If you want to accompany us to the theatre we can search that," he said to Florence.

"I'll drive there myself. I have a few things I want to do."

Looking at each other, they both realized she may try getting there before them, hurriedly saying as they were leaving.

"We'll see you there," Kadelack said.

Getting to the police car, they sped out of the parking lot before she was able to exit the building. Having the advantage of being in a police car, they arrived before her.

After Florence pulled into her reserved parking space, she opened the door to the theatre.

When she got to the office, she unlocked the door, and they went inside. She took a seat while they searched the desk and file cabinet.

"If you're looking in my office, I take it that I'm a suspect?" Florence asked.

"No, we just want to see if we overlooked anything."

"Well, I told you Cheryl's the one that did it. Did you search her apartment?"

Not answering, Davis opened the file cabinet and looked at the different folders. Taking out Carl Dunn's folder, he saw a notation where Carl had confronted Roselyn. The notation at the bottom had a date of November and read, 'Roselyn had an issue with Carl forcing himself on her. I'll have to keep this in mind for the future.' Turning the page, he read a notation from the week after Jan was killed.

"This bastard's just like Peter and some of the other men that came through the theatre. They all seem to be using me."

She noticed he was reading from her private notes and said, "If you're looking for something like a letter or character references, you won't find them in there. I don't usually keep them on file at all. If I did, I'd have to have 3 file cabinets."

Looking up from thumbing through the folders, Davis replied, "I'm not looking for anything in particular, but I see a notation here that Carl's mentioned in a way that may be able to shed a little light on this case. Is this your handwriting?" He asked.

"Yes, they're the files I start when someone gets a part in a play. I can keep track of their flaws as I see them, and help them work to improve the character they portray. It makes it so much easier than trying to remember everyone's shortcomings."

He closed the folder putting it back in its relevant order amongst the other files.

"I see. And do you always evaluate people's character if they have a relationship with you and suddenly end it?" Davis asked.

She had no immediate answer, but instead, changed the subject as Kadelack entered the office.

"Did you find what you're looking for, Detective Kadelack?"

He looked at Davis, then back at Florence.

"No. I guess that about wraps it up," Kadelack said.

Coming down the stairs from the office, Kadelack glanced back up to the office window. He could see Florence watching their every move until they were down the hall and out of site.

Getting outside the theatre, Kadelack asked, "Ben, what was that conversation about when you were looking at the folders?"

He told him what was said between him and Florence in the office, when he was looking at Carl's folder.

Kadelack said, "It sounds like she might just be a little unstable. When she told us about Cheryl having a problem taking relationships too serious, maybe she was describing herself."

"Yes. But that doesn't count for physical evidence, and I'm not a psychiatrist. With her remaining in the office, I wouldn't be surprised if she's destroying what you read. I'd like to find the gun."

Getting to the police car in conversation about what to do next, Kadelack looked over the hood. Before getting in the car he said, "Ben, I wonder if the gun was tossed in the canal?"

Davis thought for a moment. His eye's suddenly caught something, something that was already dismissed as possibly being a part of the murder.

After Kadelack opened his door and got in, Davis stood there focusing for a few moments, with the passenger door open.

"What are you thinking about?" Kadelack asked.

After Davis got in, he closed the door.

"You know, we only looked at Florence's car from the outside, thinking we might see blood. Why don't we get a search warrant and give it a closer examination before searching the canal?" Davis said.

"That's a good idea. I'll get the warrant typed up, and we can serve it today."

After obtaining it, they returned to the theatre parking lot. Florence's car was gone, so they drove to her apartment complex and saw it.

The detectives knocked once again at her door.

She opened it with less than a serene response.

"What the hell do you want now? This is getting annoying. If you want to arrest me, do it! I'm sick and tired of being accused."

"Whoa! Whoa!" Davis said, "No one's accusing you of anything. We have a job to do, and there are steps that have to be followed."

"We have a warrant to search your vehicle," Kadelack interjected. "Would you accompany us and unlock it?"

Her hostile demeanor muted, and in a quieter tone, she replied, "Sure, just a minute. They're in my purse in the bedroom. I'll get them."

"We'll be waiting by your car," Kadelack said.

Several minutes passed, then several more. Concerned that she wasn't coming, they returned to her apartment. The door was locked, and they rang the bell. When she didn't come to the door after a few minutes, Davis began knocking. Still, with no answer. He began pounding calling her name.

"Florence, open the door!" Davis yelled.

Still no response, Ben threw his weight against the door, but it didn't budge.

The metal door was the only obstacle between Florence and prosecution for her part of Jan and Carl Dunn's murder, but it was a barrier they couldn't breach.

Neighbors from several nearby apartments, aroused by the noise- came out into the hall.

One of the neighbors asked in an excited tone, "What's going on? Who are you? Why are you pounding on Florence's door?"

Kadelack showed them his badge.

"We're detectives. Do you have a superintendent of this apartment building?" Kadelack asked.

One of the neighbors replied nervously, "His office is in the other building. Why?"

"We have to get in here." Kadelack immediately replied. "Do you have his phone number?"

"Yes, you can use my phone," another neighbor said.

Before walking away, Kadelack said, "John, keep knocking. I'm going with this guy!"

Following the tenant to his apartment, he handed Kadelack the phone number of the office. After a few minutes, it was obvious there was no one there. The answering machine kicked on.

"This is the maintenance department. If you have a maintenance problem, please leave your apartment number and the building you're in. Thank you!"

Kadelack hung up the phone in frustration.

"He may be in one of the apartments doing a repair. There's no telling which one it might be," the tenant said.

Kadelack hurried back to the door. "John, do you have a tire iron in the car?" Davis asked.

"Yes, I'll get it."

Returning a few minutes later, Davis, being the bigger of the two, took the tire iron and began prying against the lock. The door gave way, but the security chain was still holding the door fast. With all Davis' might, he threw his shoulder against the door separating the chain. They quickly entered, while the other tenants looked on.

"Florence! Florence!" Kadelack called out.

Looking in each room, they couldn't find her. Davis tried the door knob of the bathroom, the only place left to search. Finding it locked, he knocked. Getting no response, he slammed his weight against the door. It swung open with such force; the door knob struck the wall, and made an indentation.

To their shock, the rug on the floor was blood soaked. Florence was sitting on a bathroom chair with her head leaning back against the wall.

She had an ashen color that proclaimed she was dead. She had slashed both wrists with a razor.

"I'll call the coroner's office and have them come out. I want to get a few pictures," Kadelack said.

Davis picked up a small bottle with his handkerchief.

"Wait a minute John. Look at this!"

"What is it?"

"The label reads 'Chloral Hydrate.' She must have taken it before slashing her wrists. Isn't that the same substance that was in Jan's stomach when she was autopsied?"

"Yes, but did Florence kill herself because we were going to look in her car?"

"There's only one way to find out. She said her keys were in her handbag. I saw it on her bed. I'll get it."

They exited the bathroom. By this time, the other tenants were actually gathered in the apartment doorway. Buzzing in quiet conversation at what was taking place.

Walking out Kadelack said, "Okay people, thanks for all your help. If you'll all please just leave, we'd like to do our work."

Getting the keys from Florence's handbag, Davis returned to the living room.

There was a knock on the open door. It was the tenant from a few doors away. Looking in the living room, she remembered the detective's from the interview.

"Officer, I'm Carol Winslow, do you remember me? I just got home. I heard there was a lot of commotion here. Is Florence okay?"

"No. Florence is dead. She committed suicide," Davis replied.

Carol looked in disbelief.

"Oh my god! Why did she do that?"

"We're not 100% sure, but we have an idea. If you'll excuse me, I have to look in her car."

Carol followed Kadelack down to the parking lot, and watched as he unlocked the door and began to search.

"What are you looking for?" Carol asked.

"I think there might be a gun in here," Kadelack replied.

As he said it, his hand hit something wedged in the back seat. Taking out a handkerchief, he carefully removed a small .22 caliber pistol.

"That looks like the pistol Florence wanted me to keep for her," Carol said.

Looking up he asked, "When was that?"

"That was the morning after I saw her and Peter coming home at 2 a.m. When I asked her why she wanted me to keep it, she said she was worried about Peter."

"Worried about what?"

"I don't know, but I only held it for her for a few days. I saw her coming in one day and told her, 'Florence, I want to give you your gun back. It makes me nervous just having it around. I'm deathly afraid of guns.'

"Did she take it back?"

"I don't think she wanted to, but she did."

"Would you be able to give me a formal statement to that effect?"

"Yes, I will!"

Getting back to Florence's apartment, he showed the gun to Davis relating the neighbor's story.

"John, it looks like the case is closed," Davis said.

"I'm sure it is, but I want a ballistics test run on the gun. If it's the same markings as the one taken from Carl's head, it's 100% accurate. I think the cast would want to know the outcome," Kadelack said.

"The next performance is Wednesday. Maybe you should call Charles and tell him first. He might just want to cancel the whole thing. While you're at it, you might just as well call Sam and let him know. Do you think the district attorney will prosecute for helping get rid of Carl's body?" Davis asked.

"I don't know. I'll have to present it to him."

After taking the gun to ballistics, it was fired and the bullet was a perfect match. That sealed the fate of Florence's guilt.

Kadelack called Charles to inform him of the situation, and he seemed relieved it was finally over.

"Charles, do you think you'll call off the show now?" Kadelack asked.

"Yes, definitely. I'll call everyone and have them meet at the theatre tomorrow morning. I'll give them the word then."

After hanging up, Charles began making calls to the cast informing them of the circumstances. He told them to meet the following morning at 10 a.m. Several people tried to pry for more information, but he held fast to address everyone the following morning.

At 10, the cast was gathered, buzzing about why Florence committed suicide.

Charles came from the office with Detective Kadelack, who informed them of what happened.

"Do to the recent events, I feel the show should close," Charles said. "The lack of attendance is the second reason. I appreciate all your efforts for making the show a success. I wish you all well in your future endeavors. The theatre will be closed for some time, until we can find another director. If you're wondering for how long, that's something I don't know."

Looking at Cheryl he said, "I'll make the offer to Cheryl here, but whether she accepts, is up to her. Again, I wish you all well."

"Well, here goes, another quest to see if I can get recognized as an actress, but in case I don't see you again, good luck!" Roselyn jokingly remarked.

"I might not be able to see you, but you'll be able to see me," Edward sheepishly replied.

After a puzzling look and a moment of silence from the group, he continued.

"I've been offered a job in advertising commercials. I'm supposed to go to New York tomorrow for a tryout."

After congratulating him, they began to disperse, chatting and talking about funny things that happened during the performances. Missed queues, Allen calling Roselyn by her real name, part of a prop falling over when Peter accidently staggered against it, funny things that kept Florence on edge. Florence. That's funny. In the short time since it happened, they seemed to have forgotten her already. Suddenly, the conversation grew solemn. Peter looked like he was in deep concentration.

"Peter what's wrong?" Roselyn asked.

The way he looked at her, she realized his thoughts were on someone else we seemed to have temporarily forgotten- Jan.

"What's next in your life, Peter? Are you still going to look for work as an actor?" Roselyn asked.

"I don't think so. This living like a vagabond isn't what I thought it would be. I called my father last night and told him I was coming home. He seemed to be happy with that and told me I could work in his company." He added in a somewhat failed Italian accent, "As they say in the movies, He made me an offer I can't refuse."

When Roselyn and Allen got back to the boarding house, they were met by Ethel.

"Ethel, it looks like you're going to lose your star boarders. The play's ended," Roselyn said.

"I assumed as much. I hate to see you two go. Oh! By the way, I almost forgot," taking a card from her apron pocket, "There was a woman here right after you left this morning. I told her you went to the theatre, and she left me this to give you."

"Did she say what it was about?" Allan asked.

"No, but she gave me money for a room for a couple of nights. You'll see her later."

After looking at the card, Allen handed it to Roselyn. Above the beautifully embossed signature was a picture of the masks *Comedy & Tragedy-* sign of the theatre guild.

"Well, here's your chance at the big time. You worked hard enough, you deserve it," he said looking at Roselyn.

"I thought I'd rather take a job helping a play write I'm going to marry," Roselyn replied.

Ethel smiled, then walked toward the kitchen. Suddenly, she turned.

"Maybe the first play you'll write; is about what just happened."

The End

Other publications by the author:

"Veronica," a fiction murder mystery that takes place in the small resort town of Beach Haven, on Long Beach Island, New Jersey.

"Mystery of the Windowed Closet," a paranormal complete with séances, psychics and unwanted spirits.

Coming in late spring 2020, *"Mist in the Blue Bottle,"* a sequel to *"Mystery of the Windowed Closet,"* the mysterious power of the blue bottle used in the séances, transcends one of the psychics into an area beyond her expectations.

Facebook – R.J. Bonett